Praise for *Laddie: A Cat's Tale*

"Delightful! I didn't know how fun it would be following a prudish English cat named Viscount Cedric of Keistershire's misadventures in America until I read *Laddie*. Bravo."

~ Bret Witter, Co-author of the #1 *New York Times* bestseller, *Dewey*

"From beginning to end, Laddie is one funny feline and cultured kitty, with his demands for 15 hours of sleep and fond memories of Venice carnival and anchovies. Arriving in America, he loses wealth and family, but he regains a different kind of both, teaching us what is truly valuable."

~ Dorette Snover, since 1997 Executive Chef-Owner of Kid Chef Cooking Camp, Chapel Hill, NC

By turns touching and laugh-out-loud funny...Laddie's whimsical adventures take him from London to New York to North Carolina. Move over, Garfield! There's a new cool cat in town.

~ Mary Beth Grover, former Senior Editor, *Forbes*

A beautiful story for readers everywhere. Kids will be drawn into Laddie the cat's world and leave with an understanding of the changing power of love. The story's action and adventure keep the pages turning, and Laddie's journey from riches to rags and back again make this a must-read!

~ Ashley Sherman, MSW, M.Ed., K-12 Licensed School Counselor

LADDIE

~ A Cat's Tale ~

Laddie

Allison Snyder
and Lucretia Herring

LADDIE

~ A Cat's Tale ~

How to Fall Off a
Cruise Ship and Land on
Your Feet

by Allison Snyder
and Lucretia Herring

Laddie: A Cat's Tale

All Scripture quotations, unless otherwise indicated, are taken from the Holy Bible, New International Version®. NIV®. Copyright © 1973, 1978, 1984 by International Bible Society. Used by permission of Zondervan. All rights reserved.

The Scripture quotation marked MSG is from THE MESSAGE. Copyright © by Eugene H. Peterson 1993, 1994, 1995, 1996, 2000, 2001, 2002. Used by permission of NavPress Publishing Group.

Pet definition taken from "Webster's New World Dictionary of the American Language," William Collins+World Publishing Co., Inc, 2nd College Edition; 1978.

This is a work of fiction. Names, characters, places, and incidents either are the product of the authors' imagination or are used fictitiously, and any resemblance to actual persons, living or dead, business establishments, events, or locales are entirely coincidental.

Cover Design: Bob Ousnamer
Cover Art: Allison Snyder and Amber Waters
Inside Illustration: Amber Waters
Page Layout Design: Dawn Staymates

ISBN: 978-1-941733-69-1

Published by EA Books Publishing a division of
Living Parables of Central Florida, Inc. a 501c3
EABooksPublishing.com

Dedication

To anyone who's ever lived with a cat and wondered what they *really* do in their spare time.

Note to My British Readers

As fellow speakers of the Queen's English, I ask your patience with the sometimes-Americanized spelling and usage herein. I live with Yanks now. Their influences abound. As I once heard it said in Manhattan, "Charley, give the poor kid a break!"

Fond regards and happy reading,

Laddie

CONTENTS

CHAPTER 1

British Prelude

My name is Laddie. I am a cat.

Surprised I can write? You shouldn't be. After all, if a Chihuaha can wear designer clothing and a German Shepherd can pose for a wall calendar behind the wheel of a car, it should reasonably follow that a British cat can write.

But it hasn't always been that way. I mean the part about my name. I have, thank heavens, always been a British cat, that most fortunate of creatures. Yet time and circumstance happen to us all—regardless of species or nationality, whether animal or human—and this is my story.

Allow me to close my eyes, collect my thoughts, and tell you my tale. Like all cats, I do my best thinking when my eyes are closed, which is a good thing, because my eyes are closed much of the time.

Twelve years ago, I was born to wealth and privilege on a country estate in England, a lavish abode much like those you may have seen in *The Princess Diaries, Frozen,* or *Downton Abbey.* I was christened Viscount Cedric of Keistershire. I am a large short-haired black-and-tan British tabby. My stripes, which fade into black and gray as they progress to my tail, are interspersed with subtle black spots, rather like a good lynx. My undercoat is a fine shade of apricot. Quite remarkable, actually. Everyone comments on the color and clarity of my stripes — tidy and distinct. Because I am so large, my veterinarian says I probably carry a touch of Maine coon cat, which could come from a distant ancestor of the former colonies. This could also account for my ready integration into American culture.

My markings have also blessed me with white gloves and ascot that show off my large, inquisitive green eyes. I heard a human once describe them as vacant, as in "Available for Rent," and all the rest of those tired clichés. *Please.* On the contrary, my eyes are expressive yet discreet, discretion being in extremely short supply with humans — I can tell you that firsthand.

But I'm not one to pass judgment. Besides, my best friends, indeed my family, are now humans. They played a major role in my rebirth; that is, how I landed on my feet. Yes, there exists a small minority who don't have the good taste to know me as I truly am, but I lose no sleep over them. In fact, I lose sleep over *very* few things.

As for my original biological family, my mother was the Hungarian opera star Catarina. In the grand tradition of famous singing divas, she was called by her first name only. This was also a matter of practicality, her surname being Von Caterwaul. Catarina's agent explained that for an opera singer, Von Caterwaul did not have quite as good a ring to it as the simple Catarina. When she resisted—something about carrying on the proud family name—the agent was more direct. "Your name up in lights? Both names would light up the entire west end of London ... and not in a good way, either."

Catarina immediately followed her agent's advice.

She also left me in the permanent care of someone else when I was about six weeks old. This is the way of cats, as you may have observed. This someone was my grandmother.

Grandmamma was a merry old tabby who, though aristocratic by marriage, had more than a bit of Italian street cat in her. I'm sure you've seen them lounging on warm hoods of cars in Rome, favoring the Ferraris parked near the sidewalk cafés, capturing the attention of diners with their carefree, confident airs. That was Grandmamma: a lover of frequent relaxation, exotic food, and high adventure.

My father, a British earl from whom I get my markings, left soon after his marriage to Catarina. I think it had something to do with the singing. But, thank goodness, there were those who were willing to pay my mother remarkable sums of money to hear a caterwaul—I mean a Von Caterwaul!

On the estate, in addition to my tutor, I had a butler, governess, masseuse, valet, chauffeur, and pastry chef. Moreover, I was surrounded by fine art, sweeping views of the English countryside, and good rugs. You could say that the first five years of my life (about age thirty-five in human years) were spent in the proverbial lap of luxury.

Then one day Catarina glided into the library of our estate wearing one of her many smart designer dresses, fresh from the catwalks of London and Milan. Catarina hated stale couture. New, exciting, disposable — that was her fashion philosophy. Pausing in front of me, paw on hip, she cleared her throat.

I looked up. *Oh, what now?* I wondered with a barely restrained sigh. Catarina never visited me just to chat. Her rare visits involved many orders — as if she had to make up for lost time — and little dialogue.

As it so happened, it was mid-afternoon. I had slept rather late and was still wearing my purple velvet dressing gown, relaxing in the library by the fire and reading the latest issues of *HELLO Catty* and *The National Cat Enquirer*.

She briefly announced that she was extending her tour to America (New York City, in particular) and that this time I could accompany her. Since Catarina always left me behind with Grandmamma, this was a most unexpected invitation.

America. Imagine that! It had always seemed a crude but fascinating place. I had never been to the former colonies. But being an adult cat, not having found my true self, and still living at home, it did seem that I should expand my horizons a bit. Thus I agreed.

Catarina's countenance brightened considerably in response.

Indeed, why not westward, across the Pond, in search of adventure?

CHAPTER 2

Manhattan

We embarked on a glittering, windy day. The sea breeze ruffled my fur, the sun shone in my eyes, and the vast Atlantic stretched before me. Grandmamma told me this cruise would be wonderful: delicious cuisine, long naps, and plenty of both. But alas, as soon as we left sight of land, my stomach began to churn, and I spent a good deal of the trip close to the railing on the main decks. My digestive tract has always been my downfall. I was bilious beyond belief.

After what seemed like months—it was really only seven days—we arrived in New York Harbor. Ah, the relief of arrival. I moved toward the stern on the lower deck and enjoyed the solitude and fresh sea air, away from my family, valet, and the jostling crowd waiting to disembark. The sight of land improved my churning stomach, but the sight of Lady Liberty warmed my heart and almost made me glad the Americans had squirmed their way free of our British oppression. And believe me, I know a thing or two about squirming free from oppression. But I'm getting ahead of myself.

In fact, so intently was I gazing upon this icon of freedom, that I did not see a porter passing by with so large a load of luggage that he could not see me. The end of an outsized steamer trunk lifted me up and *whacked* me forward, sending me reeling off the lower deck and into the harbor.

And, dear reader, let me tell you, the water was cold! I bobbed to the water's surface, spluttering and calling loudly to my valet, "Jenkins! *Jenkins!*"

Well, this proved useless as he was simply unable to hear me. The current was drawing me farther away by the minute and the ship was going slowly but steadily onward, the sound of its enormous engines drowning out my voice. The last sight I ever had of Jenkins, Catarina, and Grandmamma was them talking at the increasingly distant point of debarkation. Jenkins was lifting his shoulders and paws in an idiotic shrug and gesturing toward the cabbies. Catarina just waved her paws in dismissal. She then hustled an obviously distraught but helpless Grandmamma away from the docks.

Shocked would not do justice in describing what I felt at that moment. A smelly wave broke over my head, bringing with it some ugly possibilities. Was this all a conspiracy to get me out of the house, off the estate, and force me out on my own? No wonder Catarina had been so eager for me to come on tour with her. And that porter. Catarina had always been an excellent tipper, free with her cash whenever she wanted anything done with speed and precision.

Even now the thought of them all is enough to make my ears lay flat to my head. But I had to concentrate on other things, survival being the most immediate. Once I got over the initial shock, the early autumn water didn't feel as cold as my initial plunge. I set out toward land at a serviceable paddle. Still, my uneasiness was matched only by my fatigue. Just as I began to give out completely, a large piece of wood floated past. I reached out with my paw, front claws extended, and barely caught it. Pulling myself up, I gradually floated toward sweet terra firma.

Several large cats prowled the shore, and they looked nothing like the cats portrayed in the travel brochures. In fact, they looked downright menacing with their unkempt fur and pieces missing from their ears, likely resulting from more than a few fights. I laughed nervously as I debarked from my makeshift wooden boat and greeted them with a hearty "Hello! Cedric of Keistershire here. How goes it, fellows?"

They glared silently back at me, looking like they wanted to pick me up by my soggy scruff and toss me back into the sea. Finally, the biggest, most frightening one spoke in a gruff New York accent. "You ain't from these parts, are ya, mama's boy?"

"Actually, Grandmamma raised me. I—"

"Oh, she did, did she? Well, I can see ya take after her. Let's get him, boys."

I must confess, I thought all was lost. I cowered and shut my eyes, not desiring to see the bloodlust in my adversaries' eyes. But just as I was sure that I would be these brutes' next meal, a feminine voice came from behind the cat pack.

"Charley, knock it off! Give the poor kid a break!"

Surprisingly, the rascals scattered. Grateful beyond words, I looked to see who had come to my rescue. My eyes fell upon a very large black-and-white domestic short-hair, about Catarina's age, but not at all like Catarina. She was plump, and her green eyes looked on me with warmth. I did not fear her, yet because she had commanded obedience from those hooligans, I dared not cross her, either. She wore a simple headscarf, like my chambermaid back on the estate used to wear, and a plain housedress. Her accent announced she was a New York native.

"Where ya from, Fancy Pants?" She looked me up and down. Her loud laugh sounded more like a bad cough and belied years of hard living out in the elements.

I looked down at my midnight-blue velveteen traveling suit, now a sopping, slimy mess. Instinctively, I patted the top of my head. Just as I feared. My matching beret—gone, doubtless to the bottom of New York Harbor. That was the last straw. I began to weep bitterly.

"Aw, Fancy Pants, don't take it so hard." She enfolded me into her ample bosom and patted me with her calloused paw.

Then she gestured to a nearby bench. "You wanna sit down? Holy cats, how in the world did you end up here?"

When I finished my sad tale of the last few hours, she said, "That valet. The noive. Hard to get good help, ain't it? And your mother, well ..."

I wiped my tears and let out a shaky breath. "What do I do now?"

"It's a big city, honey, and an even bigger country. Is there some place you've always wanted to visit?"

I thought hard. She was asking about one of my favorite subjects: me. I squinted into the sun and pondered her question. "North Carolina."

"You ever been there?"

"No, but my great-great-grandfather, the Earl of Keistershire, had a catnip plantation somewhere in North Carolina."

"Well, you'll never believe this, but my brother, Rocco, is a trucker and he's leavin' tomorrow for Raleigh, North Carolina. I can probably get him to give you a ride — free of charge, even."

"Oh, that's tremendous. I never carry money."

The whiskers above her right eye lifted. "That's a *bad* habit, honey."

As she took me to her meager but welcoming home, an abandoned Dumpster in an alley behind a brownstone courtyard, I learned that my rescuing angel's name was Gertie. She offered me a warm place to sleep among the ten kittens in her litter. The lodgings were simpler than what I was accustomed to, of course, but it was dawning on me that I had better adapt or perish. We had a simple but satisfying repast of warm stew. On a full stomach, not even the noises, sniffs, and pokes of curiosity from her offspring could keep me awake. I fell into an exhausted slumber.

The delicious aroma of grilling sardines greeted me as I awoke the next morning. New York being a seaside city and all, this seemed fitting. I was famished and fell to eating with the rest of the hoard when I noticed a black-and-white short-haired male, almost twice my size, seated opposite me at the far end of the table. He bore the facial markings of a black mask, which lent him a mildly criminal air. Yet this was lessened by a jaunty red bow tie adorning his neck. He wore a matching red cap and jacket with *Rocco* stitched in scrolling letters above the pocket. He seemed to be smirking at me. I glanced down at my unkempt self. The green slime that I'd picked up from the harbor had dried and hardened into my velveteen suit. Sleeping in it had cemented numerous wrinkles into place. After vainly trying to smooth out a few of them, I returned to the more pressing matter at hand: eating.

"Good mornin', Fancy Pants!" Gertie singsonged as she came in from outdoors. "How'd you sleep?"

"Very well, thank you."

"That's good. This here's my brother, Rocco. You'd better eat up. You got a long ride ahead of you."

Rocco stood up and strode to my place. He towered over me, and his clap of greeting on my shoulder nearly sent me flying into the large bowl of sardines in the middle of the table. There are worse places to be, but still...

"Hey, Gertie told me all about your trouble."

The combination of Rocco's strength, from which I was still recovering, and his comment about my trouble—would he increase it?—left me temporarily wordless. I chose to stare at the crusty slime patches on my pants.

Rocco seemed not to notice. He simply adjusted his cap as he reached across me and snatched the last sardine. "It'll be great havin' company along for the ride," he said. Glancing at his watch, he gulped the last of his catnip tea. "Time's a wastin'. Let's go."

I dabbed hastily at my mouth with the back of my paw. No napkins were available. Gertie stood in the doorway with a hanky clutched in her paw. I rushed past her to where Rocco's truck was parked. Before I could get the door open, a loud honking behind me caught my attention. I turned and saw Gertie blowing her nose.

I hurried back to her. "Why, Gertie, you're weeping. Whatever is the matter?"

"Oh, Fancy Pants, I'm gonna miss you. Here's a coupla bucks to tide you over till you get a job and earn some money."

First, I was unaccustomed to anyone caring enough about me to weep over my absence. Catarina had certainly never done that. She had seemed only too glad to foist me upon my governess and Grandmamma. I had been a bother to Catarina and all she had wanted to do was to get rid of me. I had been a bother to Gertie yet she was going to *miss* me? Her reaction stirred something within me—a brief flash of perhaps knowing what real care was like.

But second, I was puzzled by the soiled, crumpled bills that she had pulled from her apron pocket and pressed into my paw. I stared at her blankly. Money? Job?

Well, I hadn't the time to worry about that. Rocco was beeping the truck's horn, obviously impatient to be on the road, and I had a family estate to find. I gave Gertie a peck on the cheek, thanked her for her hospitality, and hustled over to Rocco's truck.

I tugged on the passenger-side door, but it was locked. I knocked on the window to get Rocco's attention and pointed down toward the handle. But he ignored me as he jumped down from the cab. He and another cat were engaged in a heated conversation.

"I told you, Gino. I ain't got it and I won't till I get back from Raleigh."

"But, Rocco, you owe me."

"Yeah, yeah. Five hundred bucks. It ain't the end of the world."

"It might be for me if I don't pay Tony."

13

"Hey! That's not my problem. What part of 'I ain't got it' don't you understand?"

"But—"

"Shaddup!" Rocco cocked his fist and took a few steps toward Gino.

The other cat beat a hasty retreat.

"C'mon, Fancy Pants!" Rocco bellowed with a welcoming wave of his paw as he returned his attention to the truck and unlocked the doors.

I scrambled up into the cab, quite willing to do whatever he told me to do.

As we pulled away from the curb, I looked back to Gertie, her ten kittens milling about her. She waved her hanky and I waved back, not at all sure what I was doing or where I was going. Of course, I knew that I was headed to Raleigh and Rocco was taking me there, but what would happen to me then? Fear and excitement mixed within me to make a queer, new feeling of ... what? Possibility?

Before I could reflect further upon my questions, Rocco stepped firmly on the gas pedal and we were off.

CHAPTER 3

In Which I Learn
My Options

At first I wondered what Rocco was delivering to Raleigh. After all, considering his recent encounter with the hapless Gino, who on earth knew what contraband he might be transporting? Bodies? Weapons?

Oh, but now I knew. The tantalizing aroma of anchovies packed in extra-virgin olive oil filled the truck cab. Rocco opened the windows, and despite the smelly diesel fumes emanating from the Manhattan morning rush hour, I found the cool morning breeze ruffling my fur to be quite comforting.

Rocco steered us into the humming, fluorescent twilight of the Holland Tunnel. We soon passed a mosaic sign on the tunnel wall that announced we were in New Jersey. Attempting to rest, I closed my eyes and recalled the last time I'd eaten anchovies packed in EVOO. I was back in Venice. A gondolier piloted Grandmamma and me on a moonlit canal. We were enjoying a midnight snack after having prowled the alleyways during carnival. Just as I was about to sample one of the savory little fish, I was jolted out of my reverie by Rocco fairly leaning on his horn as we changed lanes in the bumper-to-bumper traffic outside the tunnel. He stuck his arm out of his window and made a crude gesture to a fellow motorist. My ears flew back from the shock to my senses, not even to *mention* Rocco's bad language.

Having finally found his desired spot in the cat lane of the interstate, Rocco broke the silence. "So, Gertie told me about your trouble. What are your plans?"

I was still recovering from the bit of road rage I'd just witnessed, trying to bring my ears back to a neutral position. As I was accustomed to neither trouble nor plans, I was rather at a loss. At the same time, I felt pressed to think fast. I could tell that he was not a cat to be trifled with and expected an answer.

"Well," I began gamely enough, "my family once had a catnip plantation somewhere in North Carolina."

"Somewhere, North Carolina. Is that a big town? Ain't nevah hoid of it. Plus, I think you might be a little outta touch with that plantation thing. Sorry, Fancy Pants, wrong century!" He erupted into raucous laughter. He obviously thought his little pun was bigger than it actually was. His accent was an *absolute pox* on the Queen's English, and he was beginning to get on my noives—I mean nerves!

I decided to study the passing scenery.

"Lemme get this straight," he continued. "The bottom line is you got no idea where you're goin' or what you're gonna do?"

I sighed deeply. "I suppose that's quite true."

"All I can say is, I'll take you as far as Raleigh." He gave the brim of his cap an idle tweak and returned his full attention to the road.

Frankly, all this talk of plans, work, money, blah, blah, blah was exhausting. I glanced at the clock on Rocco's dashboard. The only plans I had were watching the insides of my eyelids. If I were going to get my full fifteen hours for the day, I was going to have to start pronto.

The next I knew, Rocco was elbowing me awake. I yawned and stretched. I looked out the window and noted that the sun was hanging over the western horizon.

"We're here. Welcome to Raleigh, North Carolina. C'mon, help me unload this truck, if you think your white paws can stand it."

For the next hour, I helped (probably too strong a word) Rocco unload fifty crates of anchovies. I guessed this would keep the restaurant in classic Caesars for at least a year. Mercifully, the toiling ended. Rocco tossed me a tin to open so that we might enjoy a final meal together before going our separate ways. I regarded the tin with curiosity, not sure what to do with it.

Rocco crossed his arms over his chest and tapped his foot as he looked on. Then he snatched the can from me. "Gimme that, Fancy Pants." He muttered something else under his breath, evidently not for my tender ears.

After dinner, he offered some last advice. "Male to male, Fancy Pants, I'd start lookin' for a good home. I ain't so sure you was meant to fend for yourself. You might have to lose that grand-duke — or whatever it is — getup and cross over into, shall we say, the kindness of human strangers."

"Oh, I'm not a grand duke. I'm a viscount," I corrected him.

"Yeah. Well, whatever."

I remained silent. I cared neither for his smirk nor his tone, the impudent commoner. But Rocco was clearly in the driver's seat, in more ways than one. I gazed thoughtfully in the direction that I happened to be sitting, into the woods behind the Italian restaurant where we'd just delivered the anchovies. No humans there. Then I glanced back over my shoulder at the restaurant. I recalled my favorite Roman trattoria and its delicious alfredo sauce. I love rich, fat-laden sauces and am also a devoted fan of a good tiramisu.

Maybe they would take me in? I paused to process this. No, being a common restaurant cat waiting for the door to open for a few scraps, no matter how sumptuous, that wasn't me.

I looked to Rocco, who stared at me, seeming to wait for a response. I had none to give him.

He cocked his head to one side and began to speak slowly, as if speaking to someone who is not too bright.

"You're in America now. I don't know how they did it in the old country, Europe, whatever" — he scanned my appearance before rolling his eyes — "but it ain't the same here. There ain't no royalty or nobility or whatever you wanna call it. Titles don't mean nothin'. Here, you gotta work. If a cat can't make it doin' work, then ... well, that's where the humans come in."

He paused and his bravado suddenly disappeared, as if it pained him to continue, as if he needed to tell me some difficult truth. He placed his paws on my shoulders. His eyes softened. "Fancy Pants, I'm sorry, but I figure I better tell you straight up, right now. You ain't gonna make it as a workin' cat."

Pfft. Was that all? What a relief. Unloading cases of anchovies from the truck had not been particularly fun, except getting to eat some. But I kept this to myself as Rocco went on.

"From here on out, you're gonna have to be a *pet*." He looked down and shook his head, acting as if he had just dropped the worst kind of news possible.

As I allowed myself to absorb this, I wondered what the experience of being a pet would be like. Being curious as well as sensing a lack of choice, I couldn't rule it out. In the sheltered world I had enjoyed at the estate, we had had no pets. I suppose I had heard that certain humans somewhere kept some of my species in their homes. But really, what *were* pets, anyway? It certainly had never dawned on us to keep humans in the house, for goodness sake. They never seem to sleep, for one thing. Eight hours and they're done for the entire day.

Rocco drew in a deep breath and removed his paws from my shoulders but continued to lock eyes with me. "You're just gonna have to find some humans to take you in. That means you're gonna have to walk on all fours. You're gonna have to talk how they want you to talk, which means you gotta meow all the time."

He rolled his eyes again, presumably to underscore that all of this would be highly inconvenient if not humiliating. "Plus, there ain't *near* as much freedom when you're a pet. Some places won't even letcha in the door — motels, restaurants, and the like."

My stomach knotted at this news about restaurants.

"I don't see many workin' cats around here, not like up in New York. Lemme give it to ya straight, Fancy Pants. Up in New York, in my neighborhood, it's a disgrace to be a pet. The workin' cats? They'll tear ya apart." He swiped the air with claws out to make his point.

I thought about my recent encounter with Charley and his rabble. "The only upside I can see," he continued, "is that Raleigh seems to be a pet kinda town for cats. The vibe is more laid back here. I hear it's one of the best places for humans to find jobs, but we ain't in that category — human, I mean — and *you* definitely ain't in the job category. Raleigh and the area? It's what they call high-tech. Uppity, if ya ask me. You'll be right at home though."

He squinted into the last of the sinking sun and adjusted his cap. "Well, I gotta make a couple more deliveries. Then, back to New York. Got a long drive ahead of me."

"Righto," I sighed.

Rocco seemed vastly relieved, having spoken his piece. He called out the window as he pulled forward. "Don't let it getcha down, Fancy Pants. A good-lookin', smooth cat like you? Someone'll probably take you in before ya know it! Lotsa luck!"

His voice faded into the noise of the moving traffic as his truck rumbled down the street and disappeared from my sight.

I plodded back to the alley behind the restaurant. A Dumpster came into view, which briefly reminded me of the now-distant comforts of Gertie's simple home. Rocco's mocking joke about Somewhere, North Carolina, returned to mind. I was somewhere in North Carolina, all right. Raleigh, to be exact, but it may as well have been the moon. An emptiness like a vast wind swept over me. What would happen to me now? Plenty of activity was taking place around me. The distant sound of heavy traffic drifted back into the alley. Dishes clanked behind the closed back door where I now sat. But I knew no one and no one knew me.

I was alone for the first time in my entire life. My survival was fully in my own hands, and I had *no* idea what to do.

CHAPTER 4

Humans, Hotels, Churches, and Other Assorted Oddities

Human strangers?

I'd never before considered them. I'd never *had* to consider them. I did know their estate buildings were a bit larger to accommodate their size. Frankly, they'd seemed like rather dull, spastic creatures, always bustling about in their noisy ways, with their loud voices and louder—not to mention potentially flattening—cars getting in the way of a chap's leisurely nighttime stroll. And that expression "nervous as a cat"? Good grief, try nervous as a human, late and rushing to the airport.

Moreover, their brand of high energy hadn't seemed to translate into any real sense of adventure, relaxation, or how to live life. For example, many of Catarina's fans had been humans, but it seemed all they had done was clumsily and madly applaud post-performance. Cats, on the other hand, never applaud anything. Humans had previously been the distant source of my livelihood through Catarina. And according to Rocco, this would still be the case, but in much closer quarters and in a kind of day-to-day relationship.

So I walked to the front of the restaurant and set off in the direction of the nearest street sign. It indicated GLENWOOD AVENUE, which seemed to be a main thoroughfare.

I took a left out of the vast parking lot and walked up a short hill on all fours, which wasn't so bad. In fact, it seemed almost natural once I got into the swim of it. And Rocco was right. The streets were bereft of working cats. Maybe there were also no brutes like Charley? I concluded that Raleigh must, indeed, be a pet kind of town.

A renewed hope bolstered me. I was thinking of Sir Walter, the city's namesake, when in the near distance on my left I spotted what appeared to be a large hotel. In great need of a nap, I thought I might take a room. But several things occurred to me.

First, I recalled Rocco's recent advice. Did this hotel take felines? Second, I had only the two dollars Gertie had given to me back in New York. I didn't know a lot about money—still don't—but I did know that it wasn't enough to pay for a hotel room, and certainly not the five-star class to which I was accustomed.

I approached it cautiously. On closer inspection I saw that it was not a hotel at all but a church. The sign actually said so. Recalling one of my American culture guides, I assumed it was one of those Protestant megachurches. Goodness, did they sleep there too? Back home, I had sometimes tired in church, the pressure on my eyelids so great at times that I actually fell asleep. Perhaps these people had resting rooms for just such times? This was a strange country, indeed.

As I stood there in the thickening shadows, contemplating my next move, a green minivan whipped a screeching U-turn at the stoplight and careened in my direction, nearly turning me into roadkill. At home, I had always scorned roadkill, deeming it appropriate food for only the lowest class of cat. Now, I had suddenly and narrowly escaped *becoming* it. My nerves were now awash in a mixture of self-pity and panic.

As the minivan whizzed by, I noted the driver, an older human, glaring at me, her mouth set in a grim line. I thought that if this is the kindness of human strangers to which Rocco had referred, then I would have to get a job, after all. Glancing about for a place to collect myself, I spotted a bench at a bus stop. Settling underneath it, I sat back on my haunches and began to groom a bit. As my panic subsided, so did any thoughts of getting a job. A cat changes his life plans only when said life is threatened. When the threat passes, any thought of change passes with it. Humans can be like that, too, I've noticed.

I made my way back to the rear of the Italian restaurant. Though the momentary rest had helped, I was still in dire need of a place to retire for the night. I sniffed idly at the anchovy can that Rocco and I had emptied earlier, wishing for my Grandmamma, a warm cup of cream, and a rare tuna steak.

I had none of those things.

Tantalizing smells of garlic, fresh bread, and olive oil emanated from the firmly closed back door. I plodded about for a crust of bread, perhaps just a morsel of seafood—shrimp scampi, lobster, even fried catfish. Anything would do. Alas, my search yielded only a scrap of dry newspaper fluttering in the smelly breeze behind the Dumpster. It happened to be the front page, trumpeting some human disaster. I had my own disaster to deal with, and even that had to wait for now. Completely spent, I collapsed on the headlines and promptly went to sleep.

I startled awake the next morning to a most horrendous crashing sound of metal against metal. I thought the end of the world had come. I shot out of my makeshift bed and fairly flew into the woods behind the restaurant. Once I reached this safe haven, I looked back and spotted a rumbling garbage truck that had moved into position to empty the Dumpster behind which I'd been sleeping. No, not the end of the world, but trash pickup day.

Still, so many frights and jolts in a matter of hours were again wreaking havoc with my nerves—and this latest one before I'd even awoken, for goodness sake! I took a couple of deep breaths to calm myself, then glanced about to get my bearings. Numerous houses dotted the landscape ahead. They were not estates, mind you, but snug dwellings obviously occupied by humans.

I recalled Rocco's advice of the previous day to search out the sympathy of these human strangers. Then I remembered that lady in the minivan. Exactly how did one make oneself attractive to them? The prospect of depending on what seemed clearly undependable was — how to put it? — terrifying.

Before I got much further in my fearful wondering, I heard the laughter and squeals of human children and quickly spotted two of them playing in a garden, just ahead through the trees. They did not yet see me. I took several steps forward, feeling as if I were coming ever closer to jumping off a cliff, being drawn into a world from which there was no return.

The boy noticed me first. He squinted and pointed at me. "Megan, look at that kitty in the woods! He's wearing clothes. Funny clothes!"

What a rude observation.

"He's looks so tired and sad. Let's go pet him," the girl added.

They walked quietly and gently toward me, almost on tiptoes, which I found reassuring. I squinted up at them, into the morning sun.

"Aw, Billy, isn't he sweet? I don't think he's got anywhere to go."

Things were looking up. This young female was thinking of me and my apparent needs. She stroked my back and made soft, encouraging noises. I was beginning to like her more by the minute, and I hadn't had a decent massage in days.

"I dunno. We already have two cats. What's Mama gonna say?"

"The only way to know is to ask. C'mon, let's go!"

Megan suddenly scooped me up and carried me like, of all things, a human baby. I quickly checked my alternatives. There were none. I allowed Megan to do what she would. The French have their liberty, equality, and brotherhood. Hereafter my motto, in addition to food and relaxation, would have to include adaptability—never one of my strong suits.

We arrived at the rear entrance to their house. Megan trotted up a short flight of brick steps, flung open the screen door, and led the way into what appeared to be a small kitchen. "Mama, look what we found!" she reported breathlessly.

An older human stood at the sink, peeling potatoes. She peered at me and rolled her eyes. This being the second negative encounter with an adult human in less than twenty-four hours, I was beginning to seriously doubt their capacity for appreciating me.

"Not another one, Megan. We already have two."

"But, Mama, isn't he handsome?"

Remarkable taste in one so young.

Billy snorted. The older human was more verbal.

"Megan, he's a cat. And what's he got on? My goodness, and he stinks!" She drew in a little closer. "Like fish!"

It was an eau de New York Harbor and Gertie's Dumpster, topped off by the anchovies.

"If he's going to stay here, he's got to have a bath."

27

"Does that mean he can stay, Mama?" Megan's eyes were round and bright, a smile threatening to overtake her cute face.

"Well ..." The mother paused and sighed. "Maybe. First, let's see how the bath goes."

Young Megan carried me into the bathroom and began to draw my bath. I sat politely as the bubbles swirled. I wanted to make a good impression on my new ally. After all, she thought I was handsome and had said as much. She removed my wrecked traveling suit and lowered me gently into the warm, soapy water. While Megan cooed kind words, she washed away the soil and trauma of the last couple of days. Oh, blessed relief.

Then she gathered me up into a warm, fluffy towel and carried me like a baby again, this time to the kitchen where she served me a small bowl of what is simplistically known as cat food. The texture was dry and the ingredients mysterious—I detected a few stale notes of seafood and chicken—but I gobbled it down, nonetheless. She then delivered me to her room, where I promptly fell into an exhausted sleep against the soft, downy pillows of her little-girl bed.

CHAPTER 5

A New Address and
the Last Straw

Have you ever awoken because you could feel someone staring at you? Well, this was one of those times. Megan was no longer with me, but I was not alone.

Two cats were seated at the end of her bed, eyeing me in that unreadable way we cats have. You probably think I knew what they were thinking. Not exactly, but it didn't take a genius to conclude that they were not a welcoming committee. Refreshed by the recent bath, food, and good nap, I thought I'd start with a cheery greeting. I rose to my feet and took a few steps in their direction.

"Hello, chaps. Cedric of Keistershire here. And who might you be?"

They exchanged a look and then snickered. "Aren't you up there on your high horse." the larger black one said.

High sounded like "hah." I'd never heard a Southern accent outside of films, and I was cautiously fascinated. *Gone with the Wind* is my favorite, and I have a soft spot for that catty emerald-eyed beauty, Scarlett O'Hara. Still, this did seem a strange question to ask so soon into the relationship.

I drew a bit closer to them. Their mention of a horse brightened me. "Actually, I did play polo. Any clubs about?"

Well, this amused them mightily. These two rolled with laughter at the foot of Megan's bed. When the larger black one was finally able to speak, he introduced himself. "I'm Jake and this is my little brother, B. J."

B. J., still laughing—a sound like a mouse with laryngitis—only nodded in my direction.

"B. J. had an unlucky run-in with a porcupine," Jake explained. "Swallowed one quill too many."

I tried to look sympathetic, but really? Tangling with a porcupine? He needed a sanity check, not sympathy.

A sleek, muscular black domestic short-hair, Jake seemed at once tough and sophisticated. He reminded me of a chap in Monte Carlo who had beaten the stuffing out of me over a bad bridge hand. I distrusted him immediately.

He circled me slowly—I could tell this was *not* for the purpose of admiring my newly glistening fur—and then stood next to his brother. "Listen, let's lay down a few ground rules from the beginnin' of the game. B. J. and I were here before you. Therefore, we get first dibs at the food bowl and first choice of the nappin' spots. In fact, right now, you just happen to be in my favorite one."

As I thought about this, Jake advanced toward me with that wretched young B. J. simpering behind him. When Jake got within a tail's length of me, he opened his mouth and twisted his face into a gruesome display. Then he actually hissed at me!

I was stunned, but not so much that I couldn't see that Jake meant business. I jumped off the bed and hurried out of the room, a mixture of shame and outrage clinging to me.

My pace slowed as I was out of their sight and down the hallway. The humiliations of this new life were mounting almost hourly. Not only that, I was outnumbered, and while Jake was tough and shrewd, B. J. was, well, an idiot. But a coward he was not. So the remaining question was how to respond to these two.

Hmm ... ground rules, eh? I would simply need to rewrite some of them.

Before long, I had a pressing need to "go to the bathroom" as the Americans say. A stupid phrase, if you ask me: *go to the bathroom*. And then what? We cats, as you have probably noted, get right down to business in these matters. For example, at the estate, I had always simply gone outside and, well ... gone. In fact, in the elegance that is cat life, not only did this bring about relief, but it also kept the borders of the estate intact. Here, however, things were vastly different.

When I indicated my need, Jake laughed, but it felt more like a slap in the face. "We're indoor cats." He gestured to a rather small structure of sorts.

I examined it. "This cottage?"

"Yeah." Jake smirked. "It's a cottage all right. I'll call for a maid, Your Majesty, to prepare it to your satisfaction."

I had no idea what he was talking about and must have had a vacant look on my face.

Jake shook his head in apparent disgust. "Don't you have both oars in the water, son? This is the outhouse. This is where you *go.*" Clearly exasperated, he turned, flicked his tail, and ambled away.

It was certainly no house and it was definitely not out. But then I came upon a brilliant idea! I could meet my need *and* put some new borders in place, thereby putting Jake and B. J. where they belonged: anywhere but near me.

There was nothing left to do but carry out my plan. Which I did.

Well, I solved the Jake and B. J. problem but created an even more serious one with the humans. And for one who has crossed over to being a pet, this is the very *worst* problem to have.

"Megan, if that cat goes in the house one more time, he's history," I overheard from the father one day as I was strolling through the kitchen.

"But, Daddy, give him a chance."

"He's got one more chance. Then he goes."

I did not like the sound of this, not one bit. For a human, Megan's father was a fairly quiet sort who did not feel the need to raise his voice to make himself understood, which was all the more reason to conclude that he was not making an idle threat. I wondered just exactly what he meant by "then he goes." Go where?

Several days later, Megan and her father were eating lunch at the kitchen table. The sound of the front doorbell interrupted the stony silence that reigned as a result of my most recent marking incident. Megan leaped from the table to answer it. She swung the door open.

"Hi, Megan. I'm Mr. Schroder. Is your dad home? I want to make sure the new deck is okay."

"Sure, come on in." She opened the door wider to allow the man in. "Daddy, Mr. Schroder's here!"

I sauntered into the foyer, trying not to show my mounting desperation. He looked like a pleasant enough chap, as well as an opportunity for survival. He reached down to pat me on the head. "Hi, big boy, how are you?"

Oh, if you only knew, I wanted to cry out. His were the first kind words I'd received since I'd been here, except from Megan, and I knew her influence was limited. My border maintenance policies were unpopular. What was worse, my situation had now come to the point where I had heard Megan's parents talking in low tones about "what to do with Mittens." And yes, by this time, I had been renamed "Mittens." (Megan's idea.) *Gloves, my dear. Gloves!* I wanted to shout at her. Instead, I fumed to myself. One moment these humans were all fawning and smiles, the next all malice and bad taste—an unpredictable species, the whole lot of them!

In any case, such were my wretched circumstances when this Mr. Schroder appeared.

Megan's father joined Mr. Schroder and they shook hands.

"Hi, Bob. Come on in. The deck is great. Let me get you a check."

Why couldn't he spare some of that same kindness for me?

They walked from the foyer up the stairs and into the kitchen. I decided to follow this Bob Schroder fellow and introduce myself, if he'd have it. Remembering how easy it had been to win over the child Megan without even trying, I decided to see what would happen if I hit him with the full force of my charm. I simply flopped over in his path.

"Hi, big boy," he said again and massaged my belly.

Ah, such comfort! I purred and gazed up at him, narrowing my eyes as I relaxed. A fleeting flash—something like appreciation—came over me. How I longed for this seemingly appreciative human to save me from this place.

"My wife would love this cat."

"Your wife can *have* that cat," Megan's father replied without missing a beat.

Hope sprang and despair plunged within me in the span of seconds. How does a cat survive this life, I ask you?

"He's been marking inside. We're at the end of our ideas on how to get him to stop. The vet said the only thing we could do was try to find a home for him where he would be the only cat."

Sounded like heaven to me, but where was such a place?

The newcomer was now scratching my jaw and massaging my head. I could see that he was thinking hard. So I just kept pouring on my charm, continuing my solid purr and warm, hypnotic stare.

After giving me a final pat on the head, he thanked Megan's father for the check, and bid us all a good day. I trotted after him, desperation again rising within me. The front door clicked shut after him. Frozen to the spot on the cold tile in the foyer, I could do nothing but stare at the closed door, my hopes of leaving with Mr. Schroder now completely dashed. My stay at Megan's was coming to a close. The phrase *what to do with Mittens* rang through my head, but I was clueless as to where I'd go or what dire straits I might soon find myself in.

Whatever was to come next did not sound promising.

CHAPTER 6

Hanging by a Thread

The rest of the day passed uncomfortably. The floodgates of truth were now open. There was no more whispering. In fact, they were now freely discussing my next home. They called it "the shelter," and by the way they talked about it, I could tell it was not the Savoy or even vaguely like it. It didn't even sound like a shelter.

I slept little that night, except maybe a brief four-hour nap, and if you think my roommates had any sympathy for my plight, think again.

Jake sidled up to me in the darkness, purring with self-satisfaction. "The shelter, huh? Well, son, looks like you're a short-timer now. Not much call there for a salmon-and-cream type like you. And if no one comes for you in thirty days, it's lights out."

He gave his tail a harsh flick, suggesting some violent end. My stomach twisted and my paws went clammy. Mercifully, daylight came. I had no appetite.

Around midmorning, the phone rang, startling me out of a fitful sleep. Megan's mother picked it up.

"Hello?...Oh, hi Bob."

My eyes flew open. My ears perked up. That Bob fellow was calling. Megan's mother seemed pleased. There was a long pause as apparently he was speaking.

"Well, sure, if your wife would like to come over and take a look at him ..."

Him? Did she mean me? Someone wanted to look at me? My mind began to race.

"Tonight? After work? Sure, how about, say, six o'clock? ... Okay, we'll see you then. Bye." She hung up and immediately rang up Megan's father. "I can't believe it. Bob's *wife* might want Mittens. They're coming over after work! ... Yes! Can you be home by six? ... Great, honey, have a good day ... See you later."

She hung up and fairly skipped down the hall to the laundry room. Well, she needn't have been so happy about it. But I was in no position to be critical, not to mention self-pitying. I had to prepare for Mrs. Schroder.

Having found new purpose in life, my appetite returned. I licked up what little food Jake and B. J. had left for me and began to groom in earnest. I went for a natural, humble look with which to win over this Mrs. Schroder. Her husband had said, when I had proffered my belly, that she would like me. So I would give her that and more.

The hours dragged by until six o'clock. Finally, the doorbell rang. Mr. and Mrs. Schroder were right on time, bless them. Megan's mother opened the front door and greeted them effusively, ushering them into the kitchen and offering them glasses of lemonade and slices of just-baked shortbread, which they politely declined. She was so eager for them to take me, I thought the next offer might be a stay at Club Med. I sensed, however, that the Schroders were not the type to be easily persuaded.

Mr. Schroder hung back a bit, no doubt allowing his wife to experience me unhindered. She studied me for a moment. Then she walked over and picked me up like a human picks up a baby. Being carried like a baby is one thing, but being picked up like one is quite another. And there is a limit to even my sunny nature. I meowed my displeasure, not enough to be off-putting, but enough to make my point.

"Don't pick him up that way, honey. He's not a baby," her husband said.

"Well, how do you hold him?"

At this point, Mr. Schroder seated his wife in one of the kitchen chairs. He picked me up, one hand under my belly, the other under my back paws, and put me in his wife's lap.

She began to scratch between my ears. "How handsome you are," she cooed.

Oh, it felt so good to be appreciated again, especially by someone with a little decision-making power. I purred most impressively. I very nearly felt as if I were already home.

Mrs. Schroder broke my reverie. "If he marks at our house, can we bring him back?"

"No," Megan's father said.

He may as well have added, *not in a million years.* Silence reigned. Mrs. Schroder had stopped ministering to me by this time. She gently seated me on the kitchen floor. Then she retired to the living room to consult privately with her husband.

I followed her slowly, trying not to seem too interested.

"Well, Bob, I guess we could give him a chance. And if he marks at our house, *then* we can take him to the shelter."

Oh, not that dreadful place again.

He nodded and said something that I could not hear over the hammering of my heart. Then he shook his head. There was no more getting acquainted, no more scratching between the ears. I had given it my all and there was nothing to do but wait. Jake and B. J. were in the kitchen, snickering between bites of food.

The Schroders returned from their private discussion, still speaking in low tones. They turned toward Megan's parents.

"We'll take him," Mr. Schroder announced.

I nearly fainted with relief. Jake and B. J.'s ears flew back in obvious disbelief. I recovered sufficiently to savor my victory as I looked down on them from the safety of Mrs. Schroder's arms. She gave me a kiss between the ears. It was a sublime moment of triumph. I knew that she was mine, while Jake and B. J. were history.

As my new humans and I headed toward the foyer that just a day before had been the scene of dark disappointment, I could not help but think that this change of dwelling would be a step up in circumstances. I hoped living with the Schroders would not be as trying as living with Jake and B. J. Yet, other than a few minutes of massage, I knew nothing of the Schroders or their home. I couldn't help but be apprehensive of what my new home might be like.

CHAPTER 7

A New Estate and the New Me

Some discussion ensued over the mode of transport to my new home.

Megan's father made a suggestion. "Why don't you borrow our cat taxi? Just drop it off at our house sometime next week."

Hmm ... perhaps for an emergency trip to the veterinarian for Jake and B. J.? Now, don't misunderstand me. I am not generally a vindictive sort, but I would be less than candid if I did not confess that I momentarily entertained thoughts of revenge. Specifically, what could I do to that cat taxi to cause the maximum discomfort and even ill health to my soon-to-be-former roommates?

However, these thoughts dissipated almost as quickly as they came. Vengeance requires energy and resources, two things of which I was in very short supply. As well, I'm sure you know that revenge is not a gentleman's game but a futile, nasty business offering only fleeting satisfaction.

After the good-byes were said, the Schroders loaded me into the cat taxi and put me in the backseat of Mr. Schroder's large work van.

Billy apparently didn't care, as he seemed content with Jake and B. J. Megan, however, seemed a bit sad over my departure. She had, after all, been my rescuer. I was fond of her and grateful that she had done what she could for me. Unfortunately, it was not enough.

"Can I come visit him sometime?" she asked, her eyes filling with tears.

Mrs. Schroder patted Megan's shoulder. "Of course you can."

But despite Megan's good intentions, that's the last I ever saw of her. That's the last I ever saw of clothing, too, by the way. My midnight-blue velveteen traveling suit? Gone in the trash bin after my first bath. Now I had only my full-length fur coat, which I quickly discovered was profusely admired by the humans. The petting of it also seems to be a great source of contentment and relaxation to them. Bless them, I do what I can. And I never turn down a good massage.

As I peered out the cat taxi, I saw my former roommates glaring one last time through the living room window. The van pulled out of Oak Park and onto Duraleigh Road. Good riddance. The tires hummed as we made our way toward my new home.

As I considered my future that lay before me, I wondered what my new life would be like. Perhaps the Schroders had a larger estate than Megan's family. One thing was certain: there would be no other cats, and the Schroders had not mentioned children. They are very dear, but so high maintenance. I would be the center of attention—this time, hopefully of the positive sort—which held great appeal.

The Schroders chatted happily. They seemed to like each other, which was more than I could say for the inhabitants back at the estate. Several times Mrs. Schroder turned around during the journey to check on my comfort and make encouraging noises. She continued to be quite taken with me. Mr. Schroder seemed a bit more practical, but both in their own way seemed excited to have me. I gathered I was their first cat. This was a new beginning, and I did so want to impress them—without compromising my standards, of course. As I always say, never compromise your standards, no matter how much it may inconvenience someone else. But then there's that matter of survival. Always a delicate balance.

The first thing I learned about Mrs. Schroder and her prior experience with cats was that she had been raised on a dairy farm and was familiar only with barn cats—a rough, ill-mannered lot, from my experience with those on the estate. I was momentarily alarmed. What was I getting myself into? Would I be banished to the outdoors? Expected to chase mice for my meals? But then I reassured myself that I could train her accordingly, just as I had trained my servants on the estate back home.

At last we arrived at my new home. Not at all what I had envisioned, it was a townhouse and from the outside a bit plain.

Well, I reasoned, it was only going to be me and two staff, the Schroders, so perhaps I could make do.

Mrs. Schroder lifted the cat taxi out of the backseat. I struggled mightily to keep my footing while Mr. Schroder loped ahead to open the front door.

All at once, I heard dog noises coming from the direction of Mrs. Schroder's feet. I peered out the side vents of the cat taxi and beheld what looked like some sort of terrier barking and hopping, obviously excited at my arrival. Have I mentioned that I hate dogs—loud, boisterous, dirty creatures that they are? I returned the canine's welcome with a good hiss.

"Hey there, Mildred. Go home, now," Mrs. Schroder said. Fortunately, Mildred obeyed the command and ran off across a wide lawn in the direction of some other townhouse. Her owner greeted her at an open door and exchanged waves with the Schroders.

We came into a tiled foyer. I glanced to the right and saw the kitchen with a cozy adjoining sitting area that included a pair of armchairs with ottomans arranged on a stylish rug, which at first glance appeared to be Turkish.

I observed right away that, indeed, there were no children, a vast relief. I could tell this because the house was relatively quiet. Peering ahead through the crate door, I noted a surprisingly spacious drawing room—that is, the living room—which featured a large-paned window with a view of some deep woods. As Mrs. Schroder paused to switch on a light and moved us forward toward said window, I had the opportunity to fully take in the view, which was rather charming for being in the city. One of the window sections was open and screened to let in a gentle evening breeze. The only sounds I heard were crickets chirping in the woods. I spotted a lovely courtyard below and imagined draping myself becomingly on top of one of the sun-warmed brick walls, dozing at will, perhaps awakening to hunt a squirrel in the woods or stroll the grounds.

A large sage-green velveteen chaise stood in front of the window. It looked perfectly suitable for long naps. The room was also appointed with two matching sofas, slouchy looking and inviting. Lounging opportunities abounded, certainly.

Mrs. Schroder put the cat taxi down in an adjoining space, a small dining room, and opened the door. "There you go, kitty. You're home now. Come on out."

I remained in the cat taxi. Though I felt no threat from the Schroders, I had learned from the turmoil of the past weeks since my arrival in America that discretion and patience are paramount when assessing a new environment.

Her brow furrowed with obvious concern. "Come on, sweet thing. You're home now."

I had no intention of leaving the cat taxi just yet. I needed to do some things that heretofore I had not been very good at: reflection and planning. The unpleasant memories of my recent oppression by Jake and B. J. were still fresh in my mind. As I had been the odd man out with both the cats and the humans, I'd had no opportunity to assert my true noble nature. Yes, Rocco had said there was no nobility in America, but how can one change what one is any more than one can change the blood that runs in one's veins, mine being a fine shade of royal blue?

I needed to tread this ground carefully, as I recalled Rocco's forthright lecture on being a cat in America: either work or become a human's pet, the latter sounding far more attractive by process of elimination.

A human's pet? Exactly what was it? What were the expectations and, more importantly, benefits of being a pet? Yet again, my future hinged on those questions. The main conclusion I drew from my brief, chaotic stay at Megan's was that for a pet, indoor border maintenance was strictly forbidden. Beyond that, I needed to do some research. The time would come for that, I hoped.

Mrs. Schroder smiled, patted me on the head, and turned to her meal preparation duties in the kitchen. As she opened cabinets and banged pots while chatting with Mr. Schroder, I reflected on another lesson I had learned at Megan's. In the pet world, human food was sadly off limits to house cats, but one never knew what morsels might drop in one's general direction. Megan's family had been overly fond of chicken nuggets, which would do if nothing else presented itself, but I did hope for better fare at the Schroders.

After they enjoyed a quiet, leisurely meal—I detected aromas of Thai spices and shrimp—Mrs. Schroder thoughtfully arranged a soft blanket around me in the cat taxi and patted me on the head again. As I nestled in, she placed bowls of fresh food and water just outside my open door. She also placed a clean new litter box in the powder room, which conveniently adjoined the foyer. Now free from the border-requiring presence of Jake, B. J., or any other feline roommates, I noted its location and decided I would use it faithfully.

The Schroders then tidied the kitchen and retired upstairs, presumably to bed.

For the next few days, I remained in the cat taxi, meditating and napping during the daylight hours, and coming out only under the cover of darkness to eat, use the litter box, and explore the townhouse. This was a source of increasing consternation to Mrs. Schroder.

"Bob, do you think he's ever going to come out of the cat taxi?"

"Someday. He's just getting used to us, getting a lay of the land."

Mr. Schroder was very astute, I had to give him that. And what with the recent upheavals, I found myself in even greater need of sleep. So there I was, content to ponder my new position as well as patiently observe and rest, luxuries I had not been afforded at Megan's house.

On day four or so, I was completely refreshed, and it was now time to do the above-mentioned pet research. So, one afternoon while both Schroders were out, I decided to do just that and ventured upstairs to explore.

Entering the office, I sauntered across an old but attractive Indian rug, enjoying the softness of it under my paws. I hopped up on the desk. Mrs. S. is a self-described word person, and I noticed that she had, in addition to the one on her laptop, a dictionary at various places throughout the house. One was lying open on the desk, so I flipped through the pages until I found the *p* section. Hmm, *pestle* ... *pesto* (I lingered a bit over that one) ... *pet.* Yes, here it was:

> *an animal that is tame or domesticated and kept as a companion or treated with fondness, or a person who is treated with particular affection or indulgence.*

My ears flew back in astonishment. Fondness? Indulgence? I burst into unrestrained purring. This pet business would suit me well—far better than I had dared hope! I narrowed my eyes and blinked into the sunshine streaming through the window. Then, relaxing onto the dictionary, I decided it was time for a nap, but not before savoring the fact that, indeed, the possibilities seemed endless. I drifted off thinking of salmon ... or some of that Thai shrimp perhaps. Exquisite desserts. Lavish trips.

Oh, what other delights were in store for me?

CHAPTER 8

Evaluating the Staff

Well, as it turned out, the Schroders and I got off to a bit of a rocky start.

They responded tepidly at best to my midnight request for a snack, which I made via loud, plaintive meows outside of their bedroom door, accompanied by valiant attempts to push open said door. Mr. S. sleeps like the dead and so ignored me. Not so, Mrs. S. I heard her get out of bed. Finally. Well, better late than—

My relief abruptly shifted to dismay when Mrs. S. swung open the bedroom door, scooped me up, and stomped down the stairs to banish me to the cat taxi. *Of all the cheek*, I fumed to myself. This was clearly *not* like staff training back home on the estate. Mrs. S. retreated back up the stairs to her bed—without giving me my requested snack.

Persistent, open communication. Yes, that's the ticket. So I yowled repeatedly in order to register my complaint.

The result was that I heard Mrs. S.'s feet hit the floor above me as she again got out of bed and returned to the cat taxi. She again scooped me up and stomped down yet *another* flight of stairs to the basement, which I learned would be my permanent home during the nighttime hours.

While I was initially displeased — I never did get a snack — the basement turned out to be not bad at all. In fact, it was quite pleasant and much more spacious than the cat taxi. Cozy and carpeted, the basement featured a perfectly acceptable guest room with a queen-size bed, replete with a soft down comforter and fluffy pillows in which to nestle.

In the mornings, when I made my presence known via a moving, melodic meow at the top of the basement stairs, one of them would open the door and greet me with a cheery "Good morning!" along with a gentle pat on the head, accompanied by a pleasant jaw scratching. Then they'd trot down the stairs to fill my bowls with fresh food and water and tend to my litter box, which had also been moved to the basement. No, Maxim's and Mayfair, it wasn't, but then again I wasn't living that life anymore. Adaptability, I kept reminding myself.

After my meal, I would amble upstairs, where Mr. S. could always be found with his coffee and his morning reading, seated comfortably on the living room carpet. He would entreat me with a pat on the floor next to him. Of course, I would initially refuse and stroll about, perhaps greet Mrs. S., and see if anything was new or interesting on the main level. Only then would I return to Mr. S. for my morning massage.

Mr. S., I soon discovered from the diploma hanging in the office, is a mechanical engineer. This suggests a certain appreciation for all things orderly and well designed. While Mrs. S. does most of the inside estate maintenance, he does the outside. And while I've heard him say he bought the townhouse because he had no use for a lawn to mow, garden to keep, and so on, he is a diligent sort: planting in the courtyard, washing the cars, and handling general repairs. This is not to suggest that he does not know how to relax. No, we are never more kindred spirits than when he is watching a ballgame on TV while reclining on the couch and I am napping in the sage-green velveteen chaise.

After my massage, I meow at the front door to indicate my need to leave the estate to do my morning rounds and border maintenance. This meow is just loud enough to make my need known, not like the have-to-make-myself-heard-behind-this-door communication of the early morning.

And yes, I am now what is called an indoor-outdoor cat. I have heard them similarly refer to a certain dreadful carpeting in a garden catalog. As I mentioned, adjustments abound. Humans really could take many lessons from me about making adjustments, and it's not as if I don't *try* to train them, heaven knows.

But in any case, I now maintain borders and take care of my needs as I was meant to. No compulsory litter box (Mrs. S. does keep one operational in the basement for my nighttime convenience), outhouse, or what have you—just the great outdoors of the estate. And speaking of the estate, while its total size is minuscule in comparison to the one back home, there is something to be said for less bother, less distance to travel.

Typically, I start my outdoor rounds by strolling through the grass to the woods, behind the courtyard. I stop and idly sniff the breeze to determine if anyone is about. The woods are always of interest, what with the occasional squirrel, chipmunk, or mouse to chase if I'm in the mood.

And there are always the human neighbors to greet. While some pet me and even comment favorably on my looks and size, others actually shoo me away. I could hardly believe it at first, but I learned quickly to identify those I should steer clear of and those who were my fans or even potential additions to my staff.

Upon completion of rounds and border maintenance, I return to the estate to be cheerfully greeted by Mrs. S., who generally acts as if I've been gone for days. "There you are. I was beginning to wonder about you," she coos, or something to that effect.

I allow her the privilege of briefly picking me up for a gentle hug, perhaps a kiss between my ears. I even give her a friendly head bump in response from time to time. For a noble feline interacting with a human, there is always a fine line between being in charge and being a cat of the people. But Mrs. S.'s manner of welcoming me home was a far cry from any response I had ever received from Catarina, who had either ignored me completely or cast a glance at me that said, *Oh, it's you again* when I'd returned from my outdoor ventures.

And despite Mrs. S.'s prior experience with barn cats, I could call her nothing less than a quick study on what pleased me. Perhaps this came from her general background as a student. I observed from her conversations with Mr. S. and others that she attended university part time, worked outside of the estate part time, and managed the estate during whatever time was left over.

And the posh rugs and good furniture I mentioned earlier? All relics of Mr. and Mrs. S.'s past lives as well-paid white-collar professionals. Yes, they had given up money in favor of happiness and peace of mind. All very high minded, but you know that expression about timing being everything. Mine certainly could have been better. Mrs. S. is now a cheerfully cheap housewife. Oh, did I say cheap? I meant frugal.

She is a French student as well—the liberal arts type. I hear her mumbling to herself in French as she does her homework. Though I'd never tell her this, she seems a little old for homework, but she has a passable accent and has opinions about everything she reads, which I hear her share with Mr. S. She likes Hugo's poetry but adores his *Les Misérables* with its sweeping themes of grace and mercy, especially the mercy freely granted to a caught-red-handed thief so that he might not be imprisoned again, but set free to start a new life. I, too, could not help but identify with riches and a new life. But though I had been thrust into a new life, I had not yet received any riches. Well, on to Proust. She does admire Proust's idea about food reminding us of major life events. I can also relate to that, since, for a cat, every good meal is a major life event.

In fact, Mrs. S. can be rather like me in that regard. She enjoys cooking and, though somewhat petite as female humans go, she loves to eat ... and quickly. But this is one of her charms: not afraid to jump into her food with both feet, so to speak. She does use a napkin—far be it from me to paint an inaccurate or unkind picture—but she enjoys her food.

Mrs. S. is also a great admirer of Pascal. Oh, and that's the other thing I noticed about the Schroders. Like Pascal, both of them are great fans of the Bible. That morning reading of Mr. S's I mentioned? It is usually the Bible.

One afternoon I tried to divert Mrs. S's attention to me by standing on the text book she was reading. Unsuccessful, I noted the problem was that she was excited to discover that Pascal, a ground-breaking math genius and the father of the modern computer, was also a fervent Christian believer. She muttered something about how this proves that faith and brains do not cancel each other. She then concluded with no small measure of enthusiasm—still ignoring me, I might add—"Faith does *not* cancel intellect, but instead shapes it."

I said—or rather, meowed—"How interesting, Mrs. S. Now, pass me my catnip toy for some *real* fun."

So yes, my heart did sink as I realized that I had landed squarely into a nest of Bible readers. You know how tedious those people can be: high morals, self-denial, and all that. Would she put me in a plain brown woolen gown? Shave the top of my head? Impose a fast? No, thank heavens, she did none of those things. In fact, Mrs. S. did not attempt to change me too much at all. She seemed to generally accept the fact that a cat is a cat, and so be it.

One day she put me in the cat taxi to go riding in her small car with her. Alas, I grew carsick. And though I could tell that cleaning up after me was not a habit she wanted to cultivate, she never scolded me.

I did fall ill one day, and while Mr. S. thought I would "get over it," she insisted on taking me to the emergency vet. This thinned the collective wallet of Mr. and Mrs. S. considerably. She told me somewhat jokingly (her usually warm smile turning tepid), "Just so you know, you've met your lifetime medical allowance."

I took note: hit Mrs. S. anywhere but in her pocketbook.

Moreover, the vet visit resulted in a prescription. I hate pills and illustrated this to her through my stout refusal to swallow them. She would pop the little white pill into my mouth, and I just as quickly spit it out. She rang up Mr. S. and delivered this development to him.

When he came home that night, he set his briefcase in the foyer and slipped off his shoes, as usual. But he gave the living room a sweeping glance, as if looking for something specific, that thing being me, as it turned out. He studied me briefly but intensely, as if examining a solution to a thorny design problem.

Then he acted. Mrs. S. crept up behind him with something in her hand and passed it off to him.

Have you ever had someone take you by the head, force open your mouth, jam in a pill, and hold said mouth closed until you swallow? Well, I was outraged but knew I could not respond in a like manner. I was left with no choice but to rechristen Mr. S. the Alpha Male after this encounter.

And I did feel better the next morning.

CHAPTER 9

The Family

It was around this time of my first major illness that I began to think of Mrs. S. as a mother figure. Not like Catarina, mind you, who would have been informed of my illness through her personal assistant, who would have been informed by Grandmamma, who would have been informed by the chambermaid.

Mrs. S. herself had noted my condition, chauffeured me to the emergency vet, and brought me home. Yes, she was a new kind of mother for my new life. Even Grandmamma, whose attention I had placed as paramount, couldn't exceed the care and concern of dear Mrs. S.

But I promoted her to Mama the day she noticed that I entered the room like nobility. She said as much to the Alpha Male. "He's so handsome and regal, the way he carries himself. He reminds me of nobility." She chuckled a bit, as if it were amusing yet true on some level.

As you can well imagine, my heart swelled with hope upon hearing her use *nobility* to describe me. Ah, perhaps some semblance of my old life would return at last! Sensing an opportunity to prove her right and thereby assert my true nature, I raised my ears and tail and widened my eyes to display their impressive emerald color. I lowered myself gracefully onto the carpet, right in the middle of the room, so they both could see me. Stretching out my paws fully in front of me, I held my upper half erect and gazed steadily at them, first at one then the other.

Mrs. S. returned my gaze, a smile playing softly at the corners of her mouth. The Alpha Male, on the other hand, glanced at me over the edge of his laptop screen.

"Yeah, I agree," he said. "Pompous, self-important. Throw in a meaningless title. Nobility about sums him up."

A lower class of cat might have been discouraged by such insults. Not I. And besides, do you think that this was the first time? No, I had grown used to his slanderous comments by then and had even noticed that he was starting to *like* me in spite of them.

A bit of advice: always go by what humans do, not what they say. That is, examine the physical evidence: he makes critical comments about my weight, my brain capacity, my hunting ability, my bad habits, and the like, and *then* he gives me my daily morning massage. He goes out the door to work while I stay home with Mama and decide where to take my next nap.

Now, I ask you, who is the *real* head of household here?

Shortly thereafter, Mama began referring to the basement bedroom and adjoining rooms as the "ducal suite," which was very fitting (even though technically speaking, as previously mentioned, I'm a *viscount*, not a duke). So things were humming along quite nicely. Not that Mama was any pushover, mind you. Not by a long shot.

For example, when she had a break in her schedule, she'd curl up with me in the sage-green velveteen chaise, scratch my jaw, and croon, "Mama knows; Mama cares," and then just as I closed my eyes, she'd add, "Just not that much." Then she'd flash me a big smile or burst into laughter, rich and warm. Hearing this gave me a jolt of doubt, but no more. Indulgence is the best policy on these occasions.

Another time, she and the Alpha Male had just returned from the local veterinary school open house. Mama enjoys these events. They take her back to her childhood, what with all the farm animals, cow-milking kiosks, and such. Overhearing the conversation upon their return, I discovered that Mama was both disappointed and entertained to learn that "a cat's brain is about the size of a walnut."

And these humans are supposedly so smart. She obviously did not take scale into account. It might be just a walnut, but what a world inside that walnut! I necessarily developed the patience of Job for those moments. And yes, while receiving my daily morning massage, I occasionally rested on the Alpha Male's open Bible and sometimes glanced at whatever he was reading.

Job was a man who lost everything — wealth, family, health — and gave God an earful of complaint about it, yet he is given much credit for patience because he did not curse God. What would be the point of doing that, I wondered? If God is who he says he is and Job cursed him, it would seem that Job's troubles would only be beginning. But I could identify with Job, especially the loss and complaint parts. I'm still waiting for patience.

But I digress. Yes, I could go on about how Mama's sense of humor grates on my nerves or how she fails to understand me at times. But while some people in this life are merely predictable, she is faithful. I'll give her that and more. Since I have no choice but to endure her brand of banter now and then — well, worse things could happen.

In addition to her daily Bible reading, she has another dull habit. Just adjacent to my suite in the basement is a contraption she refers to as the "Ski Machine." It looks like an instrument of medieval torture. She steps into the foot straps and grabs on to some handles, which are connected to some mechanism of resistance. Then, in her mind, she is shushing for the next twenty-five minutes through a forest trail in the High Sierras.

Yes, quite.

Well, in any case, the rhythm of the skis lulls me to sleep.

I love to go into the kitchen in the early evening when Mama starts cooking dinner. My entrance cue is the sound of banging pans, which I love because it tells me that food is not far behind. However, in my position as a pet, I find that if I enter the kitchen with a persistent, demanding meow, not only do I get no human food, but I get a squirt of water in the face as well. I was *incensed* the first time this happened. As I recoiled and slapped my ears back flat to my head, my first thought was to call in my butler for the purpose of firing the whole lot of them. Then I recalled that I had no butler.

So I simply retreat to that comfortable sitting area adjacent to the kitchen. I jump up into one of my favorite armchairs — I'm partial to the one with the soft garnet-colored woolen throw — or lie on the Turkish rug. I dry my face with my paw, pausing occasionally to keep a watchful eye on Mama, till she indicates all is forgiven by either a warm smile directed my way or even a pause from her cooking for a smooch between my ears. My relationship with Mama has taught me a great deal about not holding grudges. Take your licks and move on. And if I am able to control myself, I get some of Mama's food after the family has eaten.

I particularly enjoy the roast pork, which Mama cooks simply. She puts kosher salt and pepper on it and then pan sears it in EVOO to seal in the delicious juices. Next she roasts it slowly in the oven for several hours. During this time, I am content to doze in the armchair, perhaps to the sound of a steady rain on the roof. Even as I sleep, I smell the intoxicating aromas that conjure vague, dusky dreams of my past life.

Roast wild pygmy boar ... forests of Bavaria ... thick with them ... misty rain ... travel to my hunting lodge with my staff ... I lodged ... they hunted ...

CHAPTER 10

Aunt Lu

Mama has a close friend who, by happy coincidence, has also become one of *my* closest friends. To Mama, she is Lu, but to me, she is Aunt Lu. We met through a good dessert—always an auspicious beginning.

One day, Mama decided to make a chocolate cake for Aunt Lu and her extended family in Rocky Mount, North Carolina, so she pulled out a back issue of *Gourmet* and went to work. The kitchen was soon redolent with the warm, rich scent of chocolate. Believe me, this cake included all of the best chocolate options: dark chocolate cake with milk chocolate filling and a bittersweet dark chocolate ganache icing.

The process of making this cake taxed my self-control to its limits. Mama briefly left the kitchen. Before I knew what I was doing, I jumped onto the counter, stuck my paw into the dark chocolate ganache, and began to feast. Mmmm...the luscious simplicity—just dark chocolate melted with silky-smooth, heavy cream. Surely enough to call to mind the psalmist's encouragement to taste and see that the Lord is good. Yes, thank God for ganache. But there is also a time for every purpose under heaven, and I was about to find out which one this was *not*.

In fact, my taste buds were in such rapture that I did not hear Mama enter the kitchen. But I—and probably the whole neighborhood—heard her shout, "Laddie! Get down! Get out of that ganache! You know that's not good for you!"

When has that ever stopped me? Nonetheless, I plastered my ears flat, leaped off the counter, and beat a hasty retreat. I had no desire to hang about to see if there was any mercy to be had.

Later in the afternoon, I returned to the scene of the crime and saw the finished cake on the kitchen counter, a veritable work of art. Mama arrived just behind me and covered it, knitting her brows and fixing her mouth in a grim line as she glanced down at me, obviously recalling my earlier indiscretion. She did, however, give me a tender pat on my head.

The next morning, she departed for Rocky Mount with the cake in tow. I wonder if she ever told Aunt Lu that I was the official cake taster.

Not that Aunt Lu would mind. You know how aunts can be, and I have a good one. She adores me. Mama loves me in that "eat your vegetables" sort of way. Aunt Lu, on the other hand, loves me in a "Handsome, more sausage and biscuits?" way. Yes, Aunt Lu understands me in ways that no one else does. Mama says it's because she doesn't live with me.

I've discovered that a flexible schedule is one of the advantages of being a pet, so I have plenty of time to observe the way humans talk and behave. I had become accustomed to Mama's way of speech. She is a transplant from upstate New York, near Buffalo, so her speech is quick and with lots of short honking vowels.

Then I met Aunt Lu and noticed straightaway that she speaks with a Southern accent, similar to that of Jake, my nasty former roommate. This gave me a start at first, until I realized that the similarities between Aunt Lu and Jake blessedly began and ended with the accent. But Aunt Lu does talk far more than Jake did. I've noticed that humans, particularly the female of the species, are far more verbal—dare I say, long winded?—than cats.

On the other hand, as a cat living out my role as pet, I have found a certain blessed economy of expression in the basic meow and its variations that Rocco seemed to think would be inconvenient at best and humiliating at worst. I mean, really, there isn't much you can't say with a well-placed meow, yowl, chuffle, purr, or even a hiss or a spit. But humans? Oh, how they *can* go on. They can be loud too. In fact, Mama and Aunt Lu's laughter seems to rattle the windows at times, but they are having so much fun that—well, you know me—I hate to complain.

Aunt Lu is an executive with an international Fortune 500 bank. I really like that word *fortune*. It reminds me of money. I never carried money at home because my staff made all of my purchases. I never carry money now because I don't have any. But my close friendship with Aunt Lu somehow makes up for my absent bank account.

She stops by occasionally at the end of the day to visit with Mama and me. At times, her ringing cell phone will interrupt their happy chatter, and Aunt Lu must take a business call. At these times, she favors the overstuffed wing chair in the corner of the living room. As she settles in to attend to whoever is on the other end of the phone line, I hop up and settle myself on the back of the chair, where I can listen in on what's what with her clients. Yes, I can monitor who Aunt Lu might be helping to finance that villa in Cap d'Antibes or Miami, the beach house on the Outer Banks, or the odd townhouse in Mayfair. All that talk of luxe accommodations relaxes me and I tend to drop off in mid-conversation.

Aunt Lu met Mama in a Bible study at, of all places, that former hotel that is now a church. Remember when I first arrived? The building near the Italian restaurant? Yes, that is where Mama and the Alpha Male worship, along with Aunt Lu and her husband.

And no, those aren't sleeping rooms but Sunday school rooms and offices. When I heard them mention Sunday school, I thought them a little old for that sort of thing. In my mind's eye I saw Mama and Aunt Lu wearing large bows in their hair, sitting in oversized rocking chairs. The two of them are certainly capable of any level of madcap shenanigans. But as it turns out, it is simply the part of worship where they meet with other adult humans and study the Bible and encourage one another to actually do what it says. Not that they always succeed —I can tell you *that* firsthand—but apparently there's a good deal of mercy and grace to be had in these studies, which is somehow attractive.

So yes, the Alpha Male likes me. Mama and Aunt Lu adore me. But as I soon learned, not everyone shares their good sense and taste.

CHAPTER 11

Non-Cat People

Some people do not like me. Yes, I know, hard to fathom, isn't it? But they find my entire species sneaky, selfish, and lazy.

Sneaky? I am merely discreet. Glancing at the daily newspaper, it appears that sneakiness abounds for many humans, but they make the mistake of pairing it with clumsiness. They pay dearly for this by going to jail. They lack discretion. Really, they could take a lesson.

Selfish? I am always thinking of others and how we can achieve the common goals of my comfort and survival. And as for being lazy, well, you've heard "Never put off till tomorrow what you can do today." I say, "Never do yourself what you can get someone else to do for you." The watchword here is *delegate*.

But there will always be people who cannot grasp this and thus hate cats. I won't burden you with too much about them, but all great art has light and shadow. All great literature has conflict.

And the most exquisite lemon tart can be cloying if overly sweetened.

One early Sunday afternoon as I was lounging on my beloved chaise, I heard the key in the lock. Mama and the Alpha Male had arrived home from church. But behind them, saying something about window treatments, followed a lady I had never received at the estate. My ears perked and my fur tingled at the sudden sense of déjà vu. Who was this woman and where had I met her before?

I casually strolled into the kitchen sitting area, hopped onto an armchair by the window, and looked out. Yes, it was the green minivan. I looked her in the eyes and my worst suspicion was confirmed: this was the older lady who had nearly flattened me on my first day in Raleigh.

She did not recognize me. For her and all other humans who hate my species, one cat is the same as the next. I was not insulted in the least; rather, I was grateful for my anonymity so that I could plan my next move. I kept my ears perked and idly swished my tail.

The Alpha Male gestured in my direction. "This is Laddie, Mom."

"You're right about his size. Look at that belly. He's huge!"

Madam, I'll thank you to keep my waistline out of this.

"Mercy, I don't think I've ever seen one so big. I guess he's staying?"

"Definitely." Mama stroked my head and back. "He's a keeper." She rubbed under my chin.

Dear Mama, I could always count on her.

"He must eat you out of house and home."

Oh, please.

"No, we just keep him in Techno-Diet. He seems happy."

Encouraged by Mama's kind words, I decided to take the high road and welcome our guest. I jumped off the chair, approached her, and leaned against her lower leg, giving her the rare opportunity of experiencing my fur.

"Oh, get away from me, cat," she growled as she took several steps in the opposite direction.

Again I tried the same overture of welcome.

"Cat, *shoo!*"

I knew she meant business. Still, I am long-suffering, and I decided to try again later. I told myself that just as one would patiently examine a beautiful-but-complex work of art, she just needed time to observe all of my virtues.

After they engaged in conversation in the living room, I made my entrance into the space in front of them and lowered myself upon the carpet.

She smirked. "I don't know how you keep an animal in the house."

My patience was now wearing a bit thin.

"But I know the important thing is that you like him." Her expression softened a bit as she glanced at Mama.

Well, thank heavens! At least she could recognize that not *all* people are like her in their regard for my species. Concluding that she was one of those difficult cases, I mentally shrugged and, arising from the carpet, padded downstairs to the comfort of my suite and a good nap.

Then there's Jil. Yes, that's Jil with one *l*. She has a house cat, so she apparently likes some cats. Just not me. From what I overheard Mama say, she is a German import on medical research assignment here in America. One morning, while I was out with the Alpha Male as he picked up the morning newspaper from the sidewalk, Jil stalked a considerable distance across the lawns to report to him, without so much as a good morning, that she had caught me red-handed, rummaging through her trash. Me? Rummaging through trash?

Oh, all right, so I *had* gorged myself on a half-full tin of caviar, right in broad daylight. Caviar opportunities are scarce now. Was it my fault that Jil had made it difficult to get to, buried as it was, under a pile of plastic plates, paper napkins, and a dying orchid arrangement?

The Alpha Male chuckled. "Jil, do you know how many cats in this neighborhood look like ours?"

She gave me a hard stare. I looked down, suddenly fascinated with a passing ant. As I dared to look back up, I noted a flicker of doubt in her eyes. She bid him a good day and stomped back over to her townhouse. I reflected that while I didn't like being lumped into the same appearance category as other neighborhood cats, I wasn't above clinging to the defense of mistaken identity.

Uncle Romie is Aunt Lu's husband. He once said, "One of the prettiest noises I have ever heard is the bay of a Bluetick hound when it first catches the scent."

I promptly left the room.

On another occasion, I overheard him and Aunt Lu discussing dinner options with Mama and the Alpha Male. Someone suggested sushi, to which he rejoined, and I quote, "We ain't gonna eat bait for dinner."

He also calls my relationship with Aunt Lu and Mama parasitic. Clearly, he has allowed his profession, industrial hygiene, to intrude too much into his observations of me. And I won't even *discuss* how he mocks feline hygiene with his crude, slanderous remarks. Oh, I can feel my ears going flat even thinking about it.

But I know a thing or two about difficult uncles. In England, Catarina's brother, Uncle Karl, hated me too. He enjoyed a reputation as an excellent hunter. In fact, I used to imagine him eyeing me as potential quarry. This may have been a response to my sometimes dropping fur balls into his cream. Some cats are overly sensitive to youthful exuberance, I've found.

But what do the French say? Ah, yes, I remember: the more things change, the more they stay the same. I survived Uncle Karl and I do likewise with Uncle Romie. Also, being older, wiser, and slower now, I say kill him with kindness. And failing that, stay as far away from him as possible.

Speaking of staying as far away as possible, a brief mention of dogs is in order. I've met many of them but am happy to give them short shrift by telling you about only two. The first is a Shar-Pei, those dogs with a very loose coat who could use the services of a good plastic surgeon, if you ask me. He answers to the name of Sugar Bear. That right there should tell you all you need to know, but I'll present only the facts and invite you to draw your own conclusions.

One hot afternoon in a moment of charity, I was thinking I would walk Mama halfway to the community pool, when we met our neighbor Glenda with said canine in tow at the end of a leash. Glenda is a lovely lady with a low, cultured, Southern voice, and she and Mama were chatting amiably when Sugar Bear went sniffing coarsely around Mama's pool tote. He grinned at me in that depraved way of an overheated dog. Then, without preamble, he lifted his leg and did the unthinkable, right on Mama's tote!

I arched my back and hissed at him for all I was worth.

"Sugar Bear! Such bad manners!" Glenda growled, having abruptly turned her attention downward to the commotion and then to the wet tote.

Bad manners? Bad manners, indeed. I couldn't help thinking that Sugar Bear had just marched boldly into the realm of high crimes and misdemeanors.

Glenda apologized profusely as she halfheartedly swatted the foul beast. Mama pressed her lips into a strained smile as she blotted her bag with the proffered tissue.

Then, as they apparently considered the situation further, both of them began to chuckle, which evolved into full-belly guffawing, while Sugar Bear sat there, panting grotesquely in the afternoon heat. I abruptly turned away from the whole awful scene and headed for home, thankful that our household was not saddled with such a creature.

It's truly amazing, isn't it? The discord one simple dog can stir up?

And remember Mildred, the dog who greeted me when I first arrived? As it turns out, she is a Jack Russell terrier. Mildred was a rescue dog; that is, our human neighbors saved her as she was on her way to the shelter and possible death.

Mama smiled when she shared this information with the Alpha Male and added, "Wasn't that sweet that Mildred came to live near us in exactly the same way that Laddie did? Being rescued and all?"

Good grief. Yes, exactly the same but with one important exception. She's a dog, and I, on the other hand, am a cat.

Well, in any case, she lives in a townhouse across the way, on the far side of that wide grassy lawn I mentioned. Landscaped with bushes and flower beds, this lawn is a perfect place to take refuge unseen under a bush and observe the neighborhood goings-on and, if I'm feeling social, greet the strolling humans. I probably outweigh Mildred considerably, for she is small for her breed and I am large for mine, but what she lacks in heft, she makes up for in muscle and hyperactivity. Mama has advised me to steer well clear of Mildred while her masters have her off leash as they play catch with her. It's not that Mildred hates cats, but Mama thinks she might play rough, and since I have no interest in playing rough with anything, much less a dog, I keep my distance.

But one day, as I napped through the afternoon under one of the aforementioned bushes, I awoke to the sound of Mildred's play with one of her masters. Grateful that I was well out of her sight, I took the opportunity to observe this canine pogo stick.

Notice I use the word *masters*. The humans are clearly in charge of Mildred. This one beckoned her with a raised tennis ball and she sprang up to grasp it in her mouth. After each success, she crazily wagged her tail and gazed up, eyes wide in rapture, to her witlessly grinning master, who shouted, "Good girl, Mildred! *Good, good* girl!" I glanced from dog to master, wondering who would be the first to break into a pant.

Then for variety they threw the tennis ball. Mildred fairly flew after it, captured it, and returned it to her master's feet. This little routine repeated until one of them got bored. *I* got bored long before they did. I slunk toward home, using the bushes and beds for cover. Not that Mildred would notice, entranced as she was with her joyful obedience.

The whole affair was as dull as dishwater and simply confirmed what I already knew: dogs have family who are their masters. Cats have family who are their staff.

CHAPTER 12

Names, Clothing, and Travel

I don't exactly remember at what point Mama and the Alpha Male rechristened me Laddie. I have been called lots of names by people who don't have the ability to appreciate me, none of which I choose to share here. This is not one of those sordid tell-alls that people clamor for nowadays.

I'm just grateful that Mama had the good taste to rid me of the Mittens label. Though I did have a narrow escape from a name much worse.

Around the time of my arrival, Mama worked part time for an insurance company. She saw names, names, and more names, all day long—or at least until it was time to go to her French classes. For a few days, it seemed she had settled upon Buster, after a policyholder from Mississippi. I wasn't sure I could respond to that—at least in the way Mama was hoping. So I didn't. I simply raised the fur on my back and paced circles around her at the mention of the b word. I once even sank to the level of purposely trying to trip her, but there seemed no other way.

"Buster, what's the matter with you?" she responded after catching herself.

Oh, there it was again. And what's the matter with *me*, she wanted to know? Heaven help us both, but compared with Buster, Mittens was actually starting to look perfectly acceptable.

Then one morning, out of the blue, she told the Alpha Male, "I'm thinking about naming him after one of the horses my grandfather had when I was young: Laddie."

I wasn't sure about this business of being named after a horse, but I decided it would do. Horses *are* graceful and attractive in a mammoth sort of way.

So Laddie it was. A bit common, perhaps? Yes. But it does bespeak youth, light, and playfulness, as well as "one of the lads," which pays homage to my ability to adapt to the human world.

You might have surmised by now that my only adornment, besides, of course, my full-length fur coat, is a collar. One day, Mama came back from a beach trip with a sky-blue collar covered with rainbow glitter pavé. The Alpha Male had protested that it was Carolina blue, the shade identified with the University of North Carolina; however, the Alpha Male is a North Carolina State man all the way, so he identifies with their signature shade of red. Mama, who has no sports loyalties whatsoever, ignored him and buckled it around my neck. She cocked her head to one side and studied me. You can never be quite sure with rainbow glitter pavé. Would it work? Is it too much? I turned inquiringly to Aunt Lu.

"Handsome, it's *perfect*," she said, giving my back a generous stroke. I rewarded her with a warm half-lidded gaze.

After the glitter pavé wore off, Mama got me a simple silver lamé collar. This suits me as well. I have found that anything goes well with a good full-length fur coat.

I awoke one day to find Mama and the Alpha Male bustling about the house. I lounged in an armchair in the master bedroom as Mama pulled out suitcases from under the bed. I listened as she called to cancel the newspaper. The Alpha Male entered the bedroom with a basket of laundry, warm and fresh from the dryer. I was wide awake now. They had something on their minds, and it appeared to be travel.

The air seemed thick with anticipation. Theirs was the happy, even giddy sort. Mine could better be described as dread. What about me? Who would put food in my bowl? Who would give me my morning massage? Who would smile at me lounging on the Turkish rug as she prepared the evening repast? Who would call me Handsome Lad?

I heard Mama in the midst of another phone call.

"Yes, that would be great. Just come in and give him his scoops ... OK, let me know when you're ready to write it down ...Yes, one in morning ... a little half-scoop snack around lunchtime, if it's not too much trouble. And then one around dinner time." She waved her hand. "Oh, no special time, just when it's convenient for you to stop by."

I briefly scratched my chin and fixed Mama with a stare.

"Great. Thanks so much, Brad. You're such a good neighbor. And be sure to let us know when we can take care of Athena." She nodded. "We sure will … Great! See you when we get back. Oh, and one more thing. My cousin David and his wife, Chris, will be joining us but they have to leave early….Yes, they'll be coming in one night, but it will only be for a couple of hours before they catch a flight."

Her cousin? His wife?

"Yes, they have a key … Okay, thanks again. Bye."

And what was this about "when it's convenient"? What did that mean, exactly? For example, if it were raining or if there were a good film on Turner Classic Movies, would this make it inconvenient for my dinner to be served?

And Athena. Indeed. A goddess name for that smelly old Bassett hound. Furthermore, I didn't know much about this David chap. From California, so I had heard. I had read plenty about California in one of my guides to American culture. Land of lettuce, nuts, and film stars and what have you. I had seen pictures of him around the estate, too. He looks a bit like Mama, except Mama has no Greek ancestry and no mustache.

What little I did know about him was questionable. I had once overheard an afternoon phone chat he and Mama were having. I was on the back of the couch behind Mama's head, pretending to nap but instead collecting intelligence, of course. At some point before my arrival at the estate, Mama and the Alpha Male had apparently taken a trip to his ancestral village in Greece.

Cousin Dave had said, "You can't swing a cat in Leonidio without hitting a Vlamis."

My ears flew back. I made a mental note to be especially vigilant in the event that Cousin Dave and I crossed paths. Who knew what lunatic impulse might suddenly seize him?

Before I knew it, the door shut behind Mama and the Alpha Male. I heard the key in the lock. They were gone. Well ... I had the estate to myself. I reasoned they would be back—before too long, anyway.

But I was wrong.

The first two days or so without them held a certain novel charm. The third day without them was worrisome. This Brad was spotty at best in his service to me. The morning meal was served as late as 11:00 a.m. When he finally did show, I yowled while pacing around my empty bowl to let him know that this hour was unacceptable, but to no avail. He would enter the estate, dump my scoop in the bowl, check my water supply, and leave without so much as a good-bye. And my luncheon snack? It was never served. Brad had either run out of ink while writing down the details of my care, or it was, indeed, "too much trouble." I vote for the latter.

The evening meals were just as bad. One night, he didn't come till eight, and the next night was an appetite-defying 10:00 p.m.! I was nearly faint with hunger. Otherwise, I would have given him the dressing down of his life. As it was, I fell to gobbling my food like a common dog. Perhaps I had been too hard on Athena. I wondered if she, too, had to put up with a steady diet of this so-called service.

I fell to brooding, staring out the window between naps, trying to discern how best to throw a lavish pity party for myself.

Early in the evening on day number five, I awoke to the sound of a key in the lock. I stretched and hopped down out of the sage-green velveteen chaise to stroll toward the door, relief flooding my being that Mama and the Alpha Male were home. But of course, I was not about to act like I had missed them and longed for their return.

The door opened to reveal Mama's cousin David, the Californian. It was all coming back to me now—Mama's speech about his arrival. I was so desperate for companionship that I even forgot my tail and began to pour on the charm, ears perked, tail high and curving while meowing a welcome as opposed to the demanding yowl reserved for Brad.

Cousin Dave gave me an affectionate pat, made a wry comment about my weight, and then headed downstairs to *my* bedroom, to which he obviously felt entitled. This was the last straw. I was seething. *First*, they leave me with an incompetent replacement for days. *Then* I have to bear the insults of a distant relative who takes *my* bed. I had had it. I would not take this shoddy treatment lying down. While I paced the house in the dark, said cousin and wife napped for several hours before leaving in the middle of the night to catch the red-eye flight back to the West Coast. I was left to myself again.

You might recall that I mentioned that revenge is not a gentleman's game. Well, I momentarily forgot I was a gentleman. Instead of using the cat box, I simply used the bed. The one where Cousin Dave and his wife, Chris, had slept. My bed. Well, yes I did! Cutting off my nose to spite my face, you say? There were plenty of other places in the house to sleep, and it served them right. The whole lot of them. I went to sleep on the living room couch for the rest of the night, feeling as if justice had been served with all speed and fairness.

Have you ever awoken, filled with regret over something you'd done the night before?

I loped downstairs to look at my bed. Yes, as surely as the sun rises, I had done it. Oh, what would Mama say? Or even worse, do? If she gave me a squirt in the face for whining during dinner hour, what would she do for this offense? I already knew plenty about the consequences for going in the wrong places inside the estate. Whatever had possessed me?

But then I regained my self-righteousness. What could she expect? They had all driven me to it. If Mama wanted to strive for a life of joy and self-control, that was up to her. I would find my happiness in bitterness and vengeance, and that was that.

A few hours later, I heard the key in the lock. The Alpha Male and Mama bounced in with their suitcases, all refreshed from their getaway.

Mama headed right for me. "How's my precious Laddie? Did you miss Mama?" She scratched me on my jaw and between my ears.

A jumble of emotions filled me: elation at the sight of her, desire to give her the icy treatment, and a touch of craven fear.

The Alpha Male briefly joined in the love fest. "Hi, big boy." He gave me a generous pat on my head and shoulder before walking back out the front door for another load of luggage. Those were the exact same words he had said to me when we had first met at Megan's. Guilt had joined with gusto the muddle of my emotional state. Oh, me.

I tried to keep a low profile as they bustled about. Mama approached the basement steps with a load of laundry. My pulse quickened as she descended. She paused at the landing to adjust the laundry basket on her hip. Within a moment, I heard the water running into the machine.

"Bob," she called up the stairs. "I think I'll do sheets first and get them out of the way. Can you help me strip the guest bed?"

"Sure, I'll be down in a minute ... wait, let's do the sheets on our bed too. I'll get them."

"Okay, good idea."

Yes, brilliant.

I slunk down the basement steps to the landing. There was a built-in shelf, upon which were arranged family photos. There was even one of me, lounging half asleep in the bathroom sink around the time I had arrived. Mama had thought me so witty, even adorable for having found so novel a napping spot. Perhaps, like neighbor Glenda, she would see this episode as a simple lapse of manners?

The Alpha Male jostled by me on the landing, an armload of sheets gathered in his arms. Jolted out of my thoughts, I skittered out of his way, still clinging to the relative safety of distance between me and them. He disappeared around the corner as he made his way to the guest room.

It was he who made the grim discovery. "Who—hooooo!" he hooted, followed by a loud laugh.

I cocked my head and perked my ears.

"Honey, look at the present your Laddie left for you." He sounded like he was ... amused.

Mama left the laundry room, curiosity quickening her steps toward the guest room and fixing her focus straight ahead so that she did not notice me as she passed the landing. "What are you–?" She emitted what sounded like a hybrid of a scream and a groan. I could tell that she, on the other hand, was *not* amused. "Where is he?" she asked with a growl. I had never heard Mama make that sound before.

"Honey, hold on, he's just a cat. I think he must've gotten a little nervous and anxious about our leaving him and decided he wanted to" — snorting laughter erupted and then died away when he apparently saw that Mama had no intention of joining him — "make a point."

A long pause ensued. The air was thick with tension. My collar felt tight. Maybe it was the noose I imagined was forthcoming.

Mama heaved a great sigh. "Well, you're right. He *is* just a cat. I guess all we can do is clean it up." Silence reigned as Mama passed by the landing, where I had since assumed a crouch position, to fetch some paper towels from the laundry room. Thank heavens, she still didn't see me. "But the next time we leave overnight, he goes outside."

Her firm tone indicated to both me and the Alpha Male that her word was final. No discussion. No negotiation. But outside? *Overnight?*

Mama resumed normal conversation with the Alpha Male as I crept quickly from the landing, up the two flights of stairs, and into the sunny office where I reclined on the warm Indian rug. This conflict had put me in need of a restorative nap.

I awoke refreshed after a few hours and decided to find Mama to see if she was harboring any grudges. I crept into the kitchen, reassured to find her in the midst of flouring cake pans. I noted with relief that she was smiling at me again. She picked me up and gave me a smooch of forgiveness between the ears.

Thank heavens, things seemed to be back to normal.

CHAPTER 13

The Child

Days and years passed at a leisurely pace. And despite the occasional trial, one droll comment and snuggle from Mama was followed by another visit from adoring Aunt Lu. I eagerly anticipated the daily morning massages from the Alpha Male, and I managed Uncle Romie by staying out of his way. These were the days. From my harrowing fall from the ship in New York Harbor and subsequently losing my family and all that was familiar to me, I had landed on my feet and was reveling accordingly. As staff, Mama and the Alpha Male, and at times Aunt Lu, were slow and even insolent at times. In fact, it was evident that they actually thought that *they* were in charge. But I learned forbearance (lack of alternatives is an excellent teacher) and life was humming along rather nicely.

Then everything changed.

One day—I remember it as if it were yesterday—it occurred to me that Mama had grown huge. Of course, this did not happen overnight. But that's the problem with self-absorption. You can be gazing into a mirror, admiring yourself, and the next thing you know, the house is burning down.

I won't give you all of the details of Mama's pregnancy. Female humans frequently do this, ad nauseam. It has led to many a fine nap or a demanding yowl at the front door to be released immediately. Suffice it to say that one evening rather late, Mama and the Alpha Male hustled out the door with a suitcase in tow. They came back three days later with not only the suitcase but a wailing small female bundle.

They then proceeded to ignore me with incredible zeal. Astonishing, I tell you. They even forgot to put me in the basement at night. Why, this small human could turn an entire estate upside down, what with midnight feedings, prayers that the burp would come sooner rather than later, Mama staggering flat-footed down the hallway to the nursery to pick up the Child, staggering flat-footed back to her own bed, where the Alpha Male slept in oblivion. It was exhausting to observe. How would I get through this?

One early evening, several weeks into this ordeal, I sat outside in front of the estate, on the steps with the whole family. I was trying my best to gain what scrap of affection I could. I rolled over on the sidewalk, hoping desperately for just a small belly rub.

Nothing.

I sat in front of the Alpha Male and the Child, upon whose head Mama had placed the most ridiculous-looking hat I had ever seen in my life. She was photographing them. At the moment of the shutter's click, I extended a paw of friendship to him.

Again, nothing.

His attention was fixed on gazing into the camera, an idiotic grin on his face. I gave up. I walked slowly behind the Alpha Male, my head low. The shutter clicked again. My scene faded to black as I left the estate — possibly for good. They'd never miss me. As I traipsed away from them down the sidewalk, taunting my back were their happy chuckles and the gurgles of my replacement with the stupid hat, this small and helpless human with whom they seemed hopelessly enchanted.

As I progressed down the street, my leaden heart weighed me down, and I longed for air conditioning, as the weather in North Carolina is hot and sticky in the summer months. The heat was beastly, even at dusk. I took shelter in a drain pipe, which was considerably cooler than street level but foul smelling and damp. Darkness fell. I could hear Mama calling. I was determined to teach her a lesson. Ignore me and I will ignore you. I would give her no mercy for her neglect of me. I drifted off into an uneasy sleep.

I awoke several hours later to the sound of rain and water rushing down the pipe in my general direction. Before I could move, a flood of storm water combined with sticks, leaves, and who-knows-what-else rushed over me. Carried to the mouth of the drain pipe, I dropped about two feet down into a deepening pool.

Having struggled to pull myself from it, I was dazed and depressed. What else could possibly go wrong? In response, lightning flashed and thunder pounded in my ears, which were now flat to my sopping head. I must have looked a mess.

Then I heard a familiar voice above the storm.

"Laddie! Here, kitty, kitty! Laaaddiiiie!"

It was the familiar trill of Mama's special call. She was looking for me! Well, if not actually looking for me, she was at least calling me from the dry shelter of her front door.

I hurried toward the sound of her voice. My running away from home had taken me only as far as the woods behind the house. I dashed the last dozen yards toward the open front door.

"Laddie, where have you been? I've been so worried about you in this storm. Come to Mama."

She cooed and whispered to me in nearly the same tones she used with the Child. After wrapping me in a large fluffy towel, she put me to bed in the ducal suite. I was back at the estate, Mama still cared, and all was right with the world.

I came away from this experience in the thunderstorm with the knowledge that Mama still loved me. She just had other things to do, more estate duties to manage, and the Child to care for. I needed to be patient with her. And I needed to view the Child not so much as an intrusion but as a servant-in-training. Yes, that was it! If I were patient enough, my house staff would expand to three.

But to start the training process for the Child, I would first get to know her. I watched her in her crib, all aglow like an early summer rose, just fresh from her bath, newly diapered, gurgling sweetly. She was rather cute. I continued this observation process over several months, meditating on the fact that she seemed to be a curious little thing. She was now able to crawl, and she was an insatiable grabber. Hmm. How to proceed? Well, perhaps one more good nap and then I could burst forth into the fray.

I had just awoken to find the Child approaching me. I felt a mixture of welcome—I would be attended to and cosseted—and fear. (Was a good mauling in my future?). Why had I not napped farther away from her? Where was Mama? And why was she not supervising this encounter? My eyes widened and I flicked my ears back. Panic rose within me along with the fur on my back.

The Child, meanwhile, crawled sturdily toward me, like some gleeful trench soldier advancing on the enemy. Less than two feet separated us. She was not hesitant, I'll admit that. She reached out and grabbed my left ear. Her surprisingly firm grip made any retreat impossible. *Keep calm,* I told myself.

Then she moved her other hand onto my back. She gurgled, presumably over the soft silkiness of my fur. Just as I was going to give her an appreciative blink, she took her chubby little fist, latched on, and twisted. I jumped up and yowled in protest. Thank heavens, Mama came into the room at just that moment.

After peeling off the fist, Mama told the Child, "Don't do that, honey. Be sweet to the kitty."

That's all she gets for almost having taken a chunk of my fur coat? *Don't do that, honey?* Indeed!

The rest of the day passed peacefully enough as the Child was placed in the playpen, crib, or Mama's protective lap. This training process was going to be *much* more difficult than I had thought.

More months passed. My uneasiness increased in direct proportion to her mobility. Until one day when everything came to a head.

The family sat enjoying a cozy, informal meal in the kitchen. Mama released the Child from her high chair and let her roam a bit while she and the Alpha Male returned to their meals. I lay in the foyer in front of the glass door, idly flicking my tail, admiring my stripes in the reflection. I forget what else.

Then I spotted her staggering toward me in the way of those new to the habit of walking on two legs. The next thing I knew, she was right on me. Yes, she had either fallen or dove on top of me. I couldn't breathe. In my haste to escape, my flailing hind claws caught her on the cheek. Her face turned from wonder to sadness to outrage in the span of seconds and then erupted into a piteous wail.

I heard Mama and the Alpha Male's chairs being pushed back. They hurried around the corner into the foyer, their open-mouthed looks of surprise turning into dark scowls the moment they saw the angry red welt on the Child's face.

I felt deep within me that this was it. Something would come of this and, good or bad, it was coming right then. I would either gain some additional rights around this estate or lose them all.

They quickly surveyed the situation. As nastily as I had reacted, they agreed I had had no choice in the matter, having witnessed the Child half lying on me, for pity's sake. And while not quite agreeing with me that the Child had it coming, I got away with only the rebuke of disapproving glares. I did feel a twinge of guilt, and I was grateful for not having been asked to leave. I had so much invested in them—training time and even, dare I say, some of my heart.

So I walked over to where Mama was holding and consoling the Child, hopped up on my hind legs with front paws on Mama's knee, and sniffed at the Child's bare little toes. I then gazed up, opening my eyes wide, trying with all that was within me to show my concern. Seeing the red welt did make me a bit regretful, truly.

Mama said to the Alpha Male, "Look at him, honey. I think he feels bad."

Usually unwilling to give me the benefit of the doubt, I was surprised when the Alpha Male agreed.

"Yeah, you're right." He paused for a moment before leaning down to scratch my jaw. "What else is there to do but forgive him?"

I closed my eyes in delight and no small amount of relief.

CHAPTER 14

Food, Medication, and
Personal Confession

My standard fare is now Techno-Diet Hairball Lite, laced with food pellets designed to promote a healthy urinary tract.

Yes, I know. How the mighty have fallen. A lesser cat might weep.

Surprisingly, however, the pellets are not bad, but rather tasty and high in fat. And I have not had a bit of urinary tract trouble since ingesting a regular diet of these tidbits. One very expensive trip to the emergency vet convinced Mama that an ounce of prevention was, indeed, well worth the pound of cure. In fact, Mama complained so much about that vet bill, one would have thought it was worth a metric ton.

But if the pellets have their merits, the Hairball Lite is ghastly stuff. It tastes rather like an old Christmas ornament I once sampled, but with none of the visual interest. And its very name is vulgar and overly descriptive, like so many things American.

So now you know. I have a chronic hairball problem. I had resolved that I would not resort to sordid revelation, but what can I say, now that my food and my medication are combined? Americans generally seem partial to this arrangement, what with their reduced-calorie this, low-fat that, applying to everything from lattes to steaks. I am now a permanent U.S. resident, so there you have it.

I once lounged on a newspaper article that Mama was reading about the American habit of public confession. Before Freud's "talking cure," keeping secrets was the order of the day. And then came the free expression movements of the 1960s: do your own thing, let it all hang out, and so on. Now, listening to these humans rattle on about their "issues," I sometimes long for those good old days of keeping secrets.

On the other hand, Mama, being a Bible reader, would say that confession is good for the soul. It just depends on whom you tell, the general public not being your best bet. Will you whine and complain self-righteously to anyone who will listen, thereby pouring verbal gasoline on the fire of your mental distress? Or will you talk privately to someone who will not necessarily agree with your carryings-on but listen attentively and give you the right advice? She confesses quite a lot to the Alpha Male and Aunt Lu.

The Alpha Male, I've noted, disagrees with her quite often on matters of interpersonal relations. The male of the species simply does *not* think like the female. At the time of disagreement, Mama can be irritated to no end and even throw herself into a bout of self-pity followed by a walk. Having succumbed to many of these same episodes, I am in complete agreement with Mama at these times. However, once she has had time to digest his advice, she often agrees with him and acts accordingly. Sometimes not. But either way, she does not hold a grudge — not for long anyway.

Aunt Lu, on the other hand, simply listens and Mama listens to Aunt Lu as well. They share words of comfort and encouragement, often from the Bible. Sometimes they cry like a rainstorm. Sometimes they laugh like hyenas. *They* should probably take some medication, come to think of it.

But the really meaty things, what a human would call deep issues of the soul, Mama saves for her daily time in prayer. She calls this talking to God, her Maker, getting on the same page with him, if you will. I will betray none of dear Mama's confidences, but from what I have overheard while dozing nearby, I can tell you she talks and confesses plenty.

In the early days, I would try to interrupt her with a cordial smack of my paw or a loud purr. What could she possibly get from talking to God whom she can't even see that *I* can't offer in the flesh? Still, Mama would give me an indulgent smooch between the ears and then gently remove me to her side, so that she could continue reading and talking. One day she read aloud from a psalm: "I pour out before him my complaint; before him I tell my trouble." (Him being God.)

Believe me, she milks this one for all it's worth. Far be it from me to criticize, but Mama can be a first-class complainer. But this is also probably why she doesn't hold a grudge for long. It gets poured out.

Mama once heard someone say that God can take our troubles and complaints and actually *do* something about them. Others can't. According to Mama, one could compare prayer, this talking to God, to the process of fixing something. For example, if you had a complicated instrument of some sort and there was something wrong with it, you would not attempt to fix it yourself. You would send it to the expert, the one who made it, and ask him to fix it. It would be unfair and ineffective to take it to someone who did not make it, because they would not know how to fix it correctly. Voilà, she sends her malfunctions to her Maker.

Me? I just send mine to Mama. Who needs a maker when you've got a mama?

But back to food. Not only is the hairball stuff vile, but it doesn't work.

Early one winter morning, everything was rolling out as usual. The house was bright and warm with the Christmas tree glowing in the indigo light of the cold dawn. First, the Alpha Male left home for his income-producing tasks. Then Mama and the Child bounced out the front door to deliver the latter to school. This was a workday for Mama, so I knew the estate would be quiet till afternoon. Just me at home. Ordinarily a wonderful prospect.

I awoke after only an hour of napping, with the knowledge that I was going to—how to put this delicately?—vomit with a vengeance. There are few things I dread more. Perhaps you can relate.

I tried to think of something else. But since food and relaxation are my top two thoughts, sadly, I never got past food. The inevitable took place, right then, right over the edge of the armchair, right on Mama's new carpet. I caught my breath after a fashion and felt a welcome wave of relief. After hopping down, I walked gingerly past it, took a sharp right, and headed toward the cool ceramic tile in the foyer, where my water bowl is located.

The coolness of the tile on my paws, combined with the refreshment of the water, helped me immensely, so much so that I decided to flop over onto the tile. Nothing quite beats cool tile on a bilious belly. I began to drift off again when I heard a key in the door.

My eyes flew open. It was much too early for any of the immediate family, and neither UPS nor FedEx ever enters the estate. Before I could come up with any more ideas, in through the door came Uncle Romie!

He was, as you can imagine, the *last* thing I needed. Bearing gifts for the family, he bustled by me without so much as a hello. Typical. But, thank heavens, Aunt Lu followed shortly behind and greeted me with her customary joyful noises and hugs.

"Hello, Handsome, how are you? How's m'boy today?" she crooned in my ear as she scratched my jaw.

"Lu?" Uncle Romie said quietly from the living room. "You might want to come and take a look at this."

Now, *why* would he think she would want to look at the mess I'd made? Nonetheless, Aunt Lu arose without question and went into the living room. I heard her let out something like a cross between a gasp and a groan.

There was a long pause.

"Well, we can't just leave it there. We've seen it and we've got to clean it up."

You probably think, of course, those were the words of Aunt Lu, ever solicitous, ever thoughtful of my needs and predicaments.

But no, it was Uncle Romie. I paused in my thought process, confused, caught off guard, as if expecting a snake, I was given a nice dish of crème brûlée. What *was* he thinking?

"I suppose we'd better get at it," he said, then departed for the kitchen.

He mumbled something about cleaning it up for Mama and the Alpha Male, then something negative about me under his breath which, even I, with my superior hearing, could not make out completely. I saw this not as proof of his true colors returning but reassuring evidence that he had not gone completely mad. In the meantime, Aunt Lu was looking, well, as likely to vomit as I had been before the aforementioned incident.

But I was *still* reeling from this help from Uncle Romie. Could it be that he was authentic when it really mattered, in the trenches of life when one had a disaster that needed cleaning up? Truly, Mama would not have taken kindly to having to clean up my ... um, disaster. I mean, Uncle Romie is a Bible reader just like the rest of them, but heretofore I had seen no evidence that it did him any good. That he could be a Bible *doer* was more irony than I could handle on an empty stomach.

I heard him rooting under the sink for the cleaning supplies, while Aunt Lu stood there studiously averting her eyes. She is so dear, but completely helpless where these kinds of things are concerned.

By the time the door closed behind them, the estate was once again spic-and-span. I sat in the foyer and stared thoughtfully at the closed door. Humans are, generally speaking, indispensable creatures. Odd and unpredictable? Yes, but all the same, it was becoming clear to me that I could not do without them.

CHAPTER 15

Cheating Death and a
Day at the Beach

My chronic condition put me at death's door.

Again, several months after — may I speak plainly among friends? — the barf episode, I awoke one morning feeling not quite right, but this time was different. I heard Mama open the door at the top of the basement steps, but I had not the energy to respond. This time, I couldn't even meow. I couldn't lift my head. I heard Mama's steps on the stairs.

She approached with a look of both fear and compassion on her face. "Laddie, what's the matter, Handsome?"

I apparently still looked good, which was a small comfort.

She served me my breakfast in bed. I couldn't eat a bite. She brought the water bowl. I just couldn't.

She hustled over to the telephone. "Bob, I think he's really sick ... Oh, wait and see what the day brings? ... But he has no appetite whatsoever, and you know how weird that is ... Yeah, I guess so ... All right, but if he's not doing any better by the end of the day, I'll call the vet. Okay. Bye."

So, the Alpha Male was hanging me out to dry, was he? Throwing me under the bus, to use one of his boorish expressions? I could feel my ears going flat. Mama made sure I was comfortable before leaving my room to put in a load of laundry. Then she returned to the phone.

"Lu, he looks so pitiful ... I know, that is amazing that he has no appetite at all, isn't it? ... Could you? I'd appreciate it and Laddie would too ... Okay, see you after work. Bye."

What was this "after work"? I might not be here after work! I felt so weak and nauseated, I wanted to die right there. But no, I would not give them the satisfaction. As well, I really did want to hang on for Aunt Lu. The day passed in a haze of napping interrupted by severe abdominal pain. Oh, Aunt Lu, where are you?

At last, I heard the front door open and then her voice.

"So, where's the patient?" she inquired of Mama, who was by this time making dinner.

A feeble wave of nostalgia swept over me, a wistfulness for all of those good times in the kitchen, watching Mama cook, waiting for my share. Even getting squirted in the face for yowling impatiently was preferable to this. It was hard to believe I had ever been hungry. I could hear both of them coming down the stairs.

They entered the sickroom. By this time, I could not even open my eyes.

"Lu, let's see if we can get him to eat some tuna."

One of my favorites. I should have been thrilled, but the thought of it only made my stomach do another roll.

Mama disappeared up the stairs. Aunt Lu whispered, "Just rest. Rest, Laddie. Aunt Lu's here now. That's right. Yes, you are still handsome."

Even this was not enough now.

Mama reappeared with an open tuna can. All for me and too sick to dive in. Mama lifted my head toward the can. I made no response. She and Aunt Lu exchanged worried glances. This was far more serious than anyone had thought.

"We've got to keep him hydrated," Mama said matter-of-factly.

Aunt Lu went to the medicine cabinet in the bathroom adjoining my suite. She returned with a medicine dropper filled with water.

"Perfect," Mama said, as Aunt Lu readied the instrument.

While Mama forced open my mouth, Aunt Lu slowly emptied the dropper into my parched throat. My head dropped back down on the pillow. In the dim light, I could see that a dread corner had been turned. I could hear their prayers for my survival, see that they were misty eyed, shocked over my inability to eat or drink. I remembered nothing until I awoke the next morning to Mama's touch. The drops of refreshment must have helped me rest. She was lifting me into the cat taxi.

"Laddie, Mama's here, and we're going to the vet."

Well, I certainly couldn't go on like this. The thought of getting into the car was not even distasteful to me. I was overcome by the apathy that comes with being mortally ill. I dozed fitfully on the way.

The next I knew, the vet was poking and prodding my abdomen. "I think it's a hairball, based on his history," he reported blandly. "We'll keep him hydrated and give him some meds to help him pass it."

"Well, that's a relief," Mama said. "It doesn't sound too serious. We're going to a beach house tomorrow afternoon. Can we board him here while we're gone?"

My ears perked up. This was the first I'd heard of a beach house. Beach meant Brad. And with me at death's door, no less.

"Sure, no problem," the vet replied.

"When do you expect to see improvement? When would be a good day to check in?"

"Let's give it a few days. How about Tuesday morning?"

They discussed the boarding fees, which seemed agreeable to Mama. I reflected that being sick and boarding at the vet's could be better than being well with Brad. Still, I was feeling just improved enough to be irritated over her abandoning me in my time of need in favor of a beach trip.

Mama gave me a lingering embrace as well as a peck between the ears. I turned my face away from her. *Oh, just go to the beach. I'll be fine here in the clinic, fighting off death while you frolic in the waves.*

By Tuesday morning, however, I was feeling amazingly shipshape. The previous night had witnessed my blessed relief. Not only had I passed my obstruction, whose dimensions broke records in the history of the vet's practice, but I had done so with a notable calm and grace.

I overheard the receptionist on the phone with Mama.

"Yes, Mrs. Schroder, he's fine ... No, we've never seen anything quite like it. You have a remarkable cat." She gave a hearty giggle followed by a long pause, no doubt due to Mama's expressing generous agreement with her assessment of my character. "Yes, we'll see you on Saturday. Enjoy your time at the beach. Bye now."

I was elated at my restored health and the prospect of reunion with the family. Another challenge met with dignity and strength in my new life. Lesson learned: when life hands you obstructions, respond with prayer, medication, and getting out of the estate for a few days.

Who knows? You might even come up with something record breaking.

CHAPTER 16

Gainful Employment

You have now witnessed my brush with death. But no account of landing on my feet would be complete without relating my brush with gainful employment.

Perhaps it had something to with the most recent vet bill. I remember Mama talking to the Alpha Male one evening about having seen on the Beltline a billboard of a bulldog. She couldn't recall what it was advertising—a before photo for cosmetic surgery would have been my guess—but that didn't stop Mama. "I wonder if Laddie could be a billboard or print model."

As I was middle-aged and thick waisted, I wondered how this would happen, but she had a point: if a billboard advertisement was good enough for a bulldog, it was certainly good enough for me.

She did a halfhearted Google search for modeling agencies needing cats but found nothing. I had mixed feelings. On the one hand, putting myself on display for the whole world's admiration appealed to me. Who knew that I might not recruit more staff? On the other hand, missing a nap for a photo shoot was not in the least bit attractive.

A few days later, Aunt Lu dropped by for morning coffee. I overheard Mama say, "My attempts at Laddie's introduction to the world of cat modeling have been nothing but a disappointment."

While Mama had been talking, Aunt Lu had been paying half attention, her nose stuck in the business pages. After setting her coffee cup down on the dining room table, her face wore an incredulous squint. "What did you say he had? An appointment for liposuction?"

Well, in the comic theater that is my life, apparently, they rolled in the aisles. As I guessed where Mama's coffee might end up, Aunt Lu doubled over, shaking from laughter, unable to catch her breath.

And who says I don't have a job? My job is filling their desperate need for entertainment—at my expense, of course. Well, you know what the Roman emperors used to say about bread and circuses: keep the masses fed on a steady diet of amusement and everyone's better off. Staves off social unrest and who knows what else.

Thankfully, they moved on from me and took up the subject of an old movie they had recently watched with the Child. Something about a lion and a wardrobe. Although both clothing and my distant relatives are of some interest, I withdrew from this merry gathering in the dining room and made my way to the sanctuary of my beloved chaise. Fatigued from talk of employment, having to entertain, and such, I drifted off.

Auditions tomorrow morning at nine o'clock sharp. Surely I have a chance. That vet tech had told Mama that I was no Laddie but a tiger. Tiger ... lion. They can do so much with the right makeup. She had also said I was "magnificent" – her exact word. Mama had rolled her eyes.

I found myself surrounded by all manner of my species. There was no one like me, naturally, but I did get a little anxious when I saw an actual lion. Still hopeful, I waited patiently to be called.

A coarse "Next!" broke my reverie.

"Honey, you're next." An assistant nudged me. Her accent was like Gertie's.

I entered the casting director's office. Without ceremony or greeting, he said, "Gimme your best roar."

I opened my mouth wide but nothing like a roar came out.

He got out of his chair and stomped around me. He took a couple of turns. "You'd have to get a trainer and drop some weight, but besides that, you're too short to play Aslan. We'll be doing callbacks for the part of Beaver. Call me tomorrow. Here's my card."

He flung open his office door. "Next!"

I awoke with a start and glanced around. My surroundings were just as they should be—home.

Enough of this employment business, anyway. Time for a snack to help shake off the nightmare. I loped down from the chaise and headed downstairs.

Mama ended up buying the DVD of that movie, actually. I noted that they had given the part to a lion with a voiceover from an Irishman. Some things just aren't meant to be.

CHAPTER 17

My Changing Staff

Having experienced the claw of correction from time to time, the Child treated me with a bit more respect. Pain is often a good teacher, but I had no idea how good. She fell into line so well that I wondered briefly if the same technique might be used on Mama and the Alpha Male. But then I reconsidered. They were older humans and thus disinclined to be trained by the claw. You know the saying about attempting to teach old dogs new tricks, and as much as I hate the canine reference, it is sadly true. As well, I could never persuade Mama to get on my level after having squirted me for yowling in the kitchen.

So the months and years passed and the Child grew in wisdom toward me, not to mention petting ability. Before I knew it, gone was the grabber and twister, to be replaced by a fairly competent petter and comforter, at the ready when Mama was working, studying, doing laundry, or preparing a meal or dessert. In fact, I found that with the addition of her childrearing duties (no governess, sadly), Mama simply did not have the time to minister to my needs as she had in the past, so the Child took over.

Now, this was a study in quality (Mama) versus quantity (the Child). The latter gave lots of attention, but was it the type I wanted? The answer, of course, was a moot point, which I realized one day while observing Mama, notebook and pen in hand, watching a French film for her advanced conversation class. Mama was pressing forward and taking more classes than usual in an effort to complete her last year of university. She seemed a little tired as we gazed at the screen together. The film took place in Montmartre, the winding streets, the Sacré Coeur, *les artistes.* Perhaps an interior shot of a good bistro next, a close-up of some buttery, garlicky escargots?

Or perhaps we could find the *Barefoot Contessa* on the Food Network later? Though, as near as I can tell, she looks fully shod. I think it is a reference to a carefree lifestyle to which humans so anxiously aspire and we cats so readily embrace. We enjoy her calm voice, dry wit, and her fun friends who routinely stop in at her casually elegant digs for a good feed. I have great affection for these people, since I, too, routinely show up at mealtimes.

In any case, I glanced at Mama to see what she thought. Her eyes, chin, and mouth were drooping in sleep. Shortly, her snore jolted me back to reality. I was neither in Paris nor with the Barefoot One but in the living room of my small American estate.

My overworked chief servant was sleeping on the chaise, which also happened to be my napping place du jour.

So, yes, I could reflect with some satisfaction that I now employed a staff of three. But with expansion come the inevitable headaches, and Mama's sometimes-waning energy was just one of them.

With the Child's growth came a need to control. As she was unable to control Mama and the Alpha Male due to their size and parental status, she turned to me. She developed a habit of confining herself and me in a room together. It could be any room, as long as it had a door that closed. This seemed to be for no particular reason other than the sheer sport of it. She seemed to take if not real pleasure in then a great ability to ignore my demanding yowls to be set free. Oh, she could play for hours with her Barbies—Annika, Tonya, Ashley, Adam, Abbie, Cinderella, Ariel, Lydia, and Rebecca—while I languished. Thankfully, I have a blessedly short attention span when needed, so these extended time periods often became excellent napping opportunities.

One day, however, I was feeling out of sorts. Have you ever had one of those days when you hate the sight of ... well, just about everyone? It was another beastly hot summer day, which always makes me out of sorts, and I found no relief under my shadiest bush. I was doomed to spend the entire afternoon inside the estate. So I sprinted up the stairs and sprawled onto the Indian rug in the office.

Just as I began to dream of a sleepy tea plantation in Darjeeling, Mama and the Child came bustling in and began a sewing project in loud earnest. I did my best to ignore them as Mama began sewing seams of endless length. She has a rattly old machine, a gift from the Alpha Male's mother, that she says is irreplaceable. She might want to reconsider, since it quite possibly violates a noise ordinance.

The two were chatting a little too happily. Thinking I would leave them for a quieter spot, I stood, only to discover that the door was closed. My heart sank. The Child had been one step ahead of me. I glared at both of their backs as Mama's foot appeared to be glued to that noisy presser foot. I bristled. I could feel something rising within me, and I wasn't at all sure that this was going to end well.

I got up and began to scratch on one of Mama's tote bags.

They momentarily turned from their clatter to glance at me.

"Oh, big, strong kitty. Big, strong, handsome kitty," they crooned, in halfhearted unison.

The situation had gone beyond cheap flattery, of which I am normally an avid fan. They returned to their project, callous to my needs. I would show them.

I slunk into the far corner, under the antique dining table that doubles as a computer stand, which Mama can access only by crawling on her hands and knees. Then I simply marked a border. They seemed to be having trouble knowing what borders were and apparently needed a review.

"Mama!" the Child shouted.

Mama was so busy sewing on that rattletrap that she didn't hear at first.

"Mama!" the Child repeated, pointing in my direction. Mama did a double take.

Her look could have melted steel as her fury rose like mercury in some crazed thermometer. She leaped up from her chair and ordered the Child, "Open that door!"

Presumably to throw me out.

I quickly tried to adopt a penitent posture, head, ears, and tail down as low as they could go. Then I scuttled out the open door and rushed downstairs to what I hoped was the safety of the living room. I could hear her open the door to the upstairs hallway closet, rummage for cleaning supplies, and then bang the door shut. A moment later, satisfied that I could return to the scene of my crime unnoticed and, let's face it, my curiosity getting the better of me, I crept back up the stairs. But I stopped on the landing and dashed behind the potted palm as I heard Mama's loud, still-irritated voice.

Her attention was evidently directed to some border maintenance of her own. "Press the towel hard and soak up as much of it as you can, then I'll spray the cleaner. It needs to stay there till it dries."

After what seemed like forever — it apparently takes considerable time to clean up after me — she instructed the Child, her voice quieter and gentler, "You are *never* again to confine Laddie against his will. Do you understand?"

The Child answered in a low, soft voice, "Yes, Mama."

So my purpose had prevailed. But what would be my victory's price? And could I pay it? Any satisfaction I felt was soon replaced by a strong sense of dread. Was the border issue going to rear its ugly head again, after years of bliss and peace? Flashbacks assailed me. Would Mama banish me from the estate as Megan's family had? Would another savior walk in the door at just the right time, as the Alpha Male had?

What if there *was* no other savior?

Mama remained touchy about that carpet for weeks. I could tell from the suspicious looks she gave me whenever she entered a room and found me there by myself. She would stand there and stare at me, hands on hips, lips pressed firmly together. She would sometimes bend down and check the corners of the room, pressing the carpet gingerly to see if any further marking offenses had been committed by yours truly.

But over time the grim stares and corner checks became fewer and farther between, and she was just Mama again. I was vastly relieved. Really, I had no better prospects for living arrangements. And I had grown attached to all of them. None was perfect, but each had some useful quality that I could not live without. And that thought that I had become so dependent upon the Alpha Male, Mama, and even the Child thoroughly surprised me.

How had it come to this, I wondered one afternoon while surveying the sun-dappled woods from the sill of the open living room window. Over time and through trials and errors experienced and forgiven, I concluded as a whisper of a breeze washed over me. Once these humans truly take you into their hearts, there is very little they won't pardon, very few shortcomings they will not overlook. Still, mercy is a complicated thing. By its very definition it is not getting what you *really* have coming to you. And as such, it is not to be taken for granted.

CHAPTER 18

Fame, Control, and Pet Day

I was awakened from my afternoon nap and hustled unceremoniously into the cat taxi. I learned it was Pet Day at the Child's school. Oh, that's irritating, to be shaken awake, picked up, and hustled about. Perhaps you can relate.

"Sorry, Laddie," Mama said. "There is no such thing as a free lunch. Someone else just paid for it." She snapped the door shut. "And today, it's on you." She groaned as she lifted the cat taxi and staggered out the front door of the estate.

Hmm. It was tedious at times, this world of American-style English, what with their fondness for coarse, working-class expressions. But by this time, I had grown fluent in them. The Alpha Male frequently mentioned my need to "pay my way." A smile always played at the corners of his mouth when he said this. Still, I wasn't sure what else I could not do to communicate to him that I was a pet. P-E-T. Three simple letters. Not a working cat. He had dreams of more, obviously.

Ah, what else was to be done? I sighed inwardly, resigned to Pet Day. I had overheard its description as Mama and the Child had discussed the details the day before.

"Okay, I'll have Laddie there at 2:30 tomorrow."

At least I don't have to maintain full-time employment like the Alpha Male. And they hadn't mentioned the cat taxi.

"Mama, be sure to bring him in the cat taxi, because there will be dogs there, and you know how that goes," she singsonged.

Oh, for pity's sake. I would have to endure a nauseating ten-minute trip to her school, followed by at least a half hour in the company of barely restrained yapping dogs, not to mention the barely restrained savag—I mean, children.

"And when it's my turn," the Child continued, "I get to show Laddie to the kids and give a few facts about him: that he's a mammal and what I like about him and why a cat is a good pet."

Listen, people. I don't parade *you* around in front of other cats and tell them you're mammals and explain why you make good servants. Indeed. Well, at least I would have some time in the spotlight. Perhaps even gain more fans. The likelihood of recruiting more staff seemed increasingly distant. And in the event that the dogs and children became a bit too physical, I would have the sanctuary of the cat taxi. Best to try to find a silver lining in an otherwise dreadful situation.

Mama jostled me into the backseat of her car. She pulled out onto Wycliff Road. The turns are the worst, inspiring in me a piteous yowl in time to the churning of my stomach while Mama studiously ignores me. But once we get underway on the Beltline straightaway, my condition usually improves.

The vehicle slowed when Mama pulled into the crowded parking lot of Mercy Christian School. *Mercy.* What a wonderful name. As you know, I'm all for mercy, especially when I'm on the receiving end.

Best be at it. Mama picked up the cat taxi and staggered toward the display space, which was a roped-off area of the asphalt parking lot. The Child had said that there were no pets allowed inside the school building. Something about health regulations. Can you imagine that? What about *my* health? After my indignation passed, I reasoned that being outside would be best for me. After a car trip, I require plenty of fresh air.

Mama made our way to the end of the asphalt parking lot where there were cages of various sizes containing other cats, hamsters, gerbils, and reptiles. Of course, the dogs were everywhere, jumping about and panting, as is their way, which made me think of Mildred, my Jack Russell terrier neighbor. Yes, I know that we are to love our neighbors as ourselves. But for me to love any canine neighbor would constitute a bona fide miracle, something like Jesus walking on water, in fact.

I slunk to the extreme rear of the cat taxi and listened to the various descriptions of those in the queue ahead of the Child. It seemed they were removing each pet from its cage to give everyone a good look and, if they wanted, a touch or a quick pat.

"My pet is a lizard," a lad said. "His name is Emerald. He is cold-blooded and he is a reptile. He is a good pet because he is cool-looking and he lets me pick him up."

You have exceedingly low standards, my boy. Next?

"My pet is a hamster," another said. "His name is Chubby. He is a mammal. He is a good pet because he lets me snuggle him and pick him up. He is just a baby now."

Chubby ... hmm. I moved to the front of the cat taxi for a look. He was rather plump at that. I fixed him with a predatory gaze. My mouth began to water. I licked my chops while appraising his worthiness as a light snack. But not wanting to make a scene, I abandoned further thoughts of an ambush. The poor creature looked a bit disoriented over all the unwelcome attention, and there was a rustic-but-savory meat loaf awaiting me at home that evening.

We were on.

The Child opened the door to the cat taxi and beckoned me out. As I made my entrance, a delighted gasp went up from the crowd of children.

"He's so big!" cried one.

"He's gigantic!" exclaimed another.

"His stripes are so pretty," cooed a little girl with braids. "And I love his big green eyes."

I returned her admiration with a slow blink and my tail held high.

It was a defining moment. At last, I understood why Catarina had so often sought center stage, why she had so often left me in the care of others. As I stepped forward, my tail still high and now elegantly curved, my emotions were in turmoil. The fear, the adoration, my needs, their yearnings. A cat could get used to this.

"My cat's name is Laddie," the Child spoke above the fray of barking dogs and clamoring children. "He is a mammal. He is a good pet because he's like having a tiger who does not want to eat you, and he snuggles with you."

Well, that was rather sweet of her.

"I wish I had a cat like that," one child chimed in.

The mob of children began to advance on me to get in a pat. Looking up at them—they were, after all, much taller than I—it was rather terrifying, what with their grasping hands and laughing faces, some still wearing the remnants of lunch. There were a half dozen or so who were able to simultaneously touch me. Pat. Tug. Pet. Pull. Ouch! Now I could also see why Catarina had so detested the clicking paparazzi and the ever-present chaos of the fans. All that adoration seems wonderful unless one actually has to endure it.

"Okay, children, he's getting a little nervous," announced the Child's teacher. "See, his ears are going flat and his eyes are as big as saucers."

Catarina used to look like that, too, I recalled.

The Child hustled me back into the cat taxi.

The next pet in the queue was a fluffy golden retriever puppy named Pooh. All eyes and hands were now upon him. He jumped up and licked their faces, lapping up the cheap affection of the crowd with wild abandon. Eyes narrowed, I sniffed the air. How predictable.

The teacher thanked everyone for bringing their pets and directed them back to the classroom to pick up their backpacks.

"Sweetie, I guess it's time to get Laddie in the car?" I heard Mama inquire of the Child.

"Yup. See you in carpool, Mama!"

The Child scampered off with the rest of the class, and Mama again lurched back to the car with me. As I scrambled for solid footing within the confines of the cat taxi, I found myself wishing she'd come up the learning curve of transporting me a bit more quickly.

She lowered me onto the backseat. "Finally," she grumbled under her breath.

Yes, my thoughts exactly.

I could feel the car easing into line and the delicate hum of the engine as Mama put the car into park.

Fame. Control. I considered them as we awaited the Child. Both are certainly fleeting, I reflected as I settled back into the cat taxi. Fame lasts only as long as it takes for the next pretty face to come along, and then all that remains are family and one's principles, both being adjustable for a cat, depending on circumstance.

As for me, I leave the principles to Mama and the Alpha Male. This is their strength, and I'm glad they have them. Were it not for those principles of mercy and grace to which they are so attached, I might not be here.

And control? It came to me that the family's control over me was perhaps even a good thing at times. For example, what would I have done without Mama and the Child shepherding me through the pandemonium of Pet Day? Yes, one could make the argument that were it not for them, I would not have had to endure Pet Day to begin with. But absent Pet Day, I would not have come to those understandings about Catarina.

The Child pulled open the car door, hopped into the front seat, and she and Mama exchanged smiles as Mama pulled forward and we headed for home. Life is a curious journey, I reflected. One door closes behind you just as another opens ahead.

CHAPTER 19

Rusty Hurdman

Among the things I've learned in this life is that forgiveness does not erase consequences.

Mama, Alpha Male, and the Child began packing again. Did these people never stay home? How much time off did they think they deserved? This once-every-few-years business had to stop.

Which leads to another aspect about this occupation of being a pet. Your family wants you, but typically no one else does. When Rocco had regaled me with the inconveniences associated with being a pet, he had failed to mention this one: being left behind during family vacations. But as I pondered this fact, it dawned on me that in order to go with them, I would have to ride for long periods of time in their small car.

Hmm. I would learn to be content staying at the estate.

The instructions to Brad (I sighed inwardly at the mention of his name) were substantially different this time as they spoke on the telephone.

"Yes, that's right. He's got to stay outside all of the time. His food and water will be in the courtyard...Oh yes, his cat taxi will be out there, too, door open for whenever he wants to use it."

Mama went on to explain in graphic detail all I had done during their previous absence. She could even laugh about it now. But she stood firm on the outside rule.

"If it pours down rain and it gets cold, yes, he can come in then. But only during part of the day. He's not allowed in overnight ... No, don't worry." She shook her head and waved her hand. "He never goes near the street ... Yes, he has an unfailing instinct for self-preservation." We exchanged stares.

Well, she was right about that. The street held absolutely no appeal. Furthermore, I decided then and there that I would not sink into an abyss of self-pity. I saw where that had led. No, in acceptance lies peace, and if I were going to sleep rough and dine alfresco, I would make the best of it.

The next morning, after their coffee and my breakfast and massage, Mama, the Alpha Male, and the Child finished hauling the luggage to their car. By the time they completed their pre-trip chores of canceling the newspaper, chatting with neighbors, and filling my food and water bowls in the courtyard, it was after noon. They mentioned something about lunch on the road. Mama picked me up and held me close. I don't really like being picked up—too confining. But for Mama, I displayed remarkable forbearance and even managed to purr.

She looked me squarely in the eye. "It's for the best, Laddie."

Yes, but whose best? I meowed back.

I kept reminding myself that there was no sense in being embittered and decided not to hold a grudge. Acting out past resentments had gotten me nothing but a round-trip ticket to the great outdoors, with the return date wide open. More of the same bore the possibility of bringing much worse. I watched the car as it made a left onto the street. The Child waved at me from the window of the car as it disappeared around the corner.

After lowering myself onto the soft grass of the front yard, I noticed in the distance across the common area lawn Mildred the Jack Russell and her master as they came out their front door for a walk. Mildred made her way across the parking area at the end of her leash, her gait something between a prance and a strut. Good grief, she was not only glad but *proud* to be owned. While her master paused to tie his shoelace, Mildred gazed at him, obvious adoration in her eyes, willing to wait however long it took, her tail wagging all the while. The shoelace tying done, off they went together.

I began to bat idly at passing bugs. All this excitement was almost more than I could bear. I sighed deeply and lowered my head. But then I caught a foreign scent on the cool autumn breeze: a trespasser.

My gaze followed the direction from which the scent was coming. Down the walk swaggered a smallish but muscular young orange tabby with no collar. He held a bit of an air of that Charley from New York City. Then again, maybe a little of that orange tabby in *Breakfast at Tiffany's* (who was not a good match for the lovely Audrey Hepburn, by the way). Where was casting when he got the part? Orange is much too rough and livid; think construction barrels, traffic cones, and bad polyester clothing. It also clashes with my eyes. Nevertheless, orange polyester does rear its ugly head in the fashion cycle from time to time, and here it was again.

I had learned a thing or two about dealing with these common cats. Having tried the gentlemanly route and been rebuffed and dominated, I arose and strode purposefully toward him. I wasn't yet sure exactly what that purpose was, but I knew I must come across masterfully from the start.

I got within a tail's length of him and casually sniffed the breeze.

"May I help you?" I inquired firmly, unafraid to meet his golden but steely gaze.

"Yeah, as a matter of fact you may." His body language indicated he was sizing me up but unwilling to engage. And, good heavens, his accent indicated he was from somewhere in the Northeast.

Oh, not *another* Yankee. This one transplanted. Would it never end? I had often heard this same mournful refrain from natives of the South and felt a brief pang of sympathy with them. But I thought of dear transplanted Mama. Then Gertie. Then I thought of how Mama and Aunt Lu are just like sisters. Probably all that Bible reading and taking the low place. Perhaps I was being hasty.

But this was neither the time nor the place to examine my prejudices.

"Well, state your business, sir, and make it brief."

"The name's Rusty, Rusty Hurdman. I'm from New Jersey."

Hoidman. Joisey. I cringed.

He gave me the once-over. "Got somethin' in your eye?"

"No!" I hissed.

He took a step back.

"Hey, just askin'. Don't get your tail in a twist."

He circled me, lingering when he got directly behind me, out of my line of sight. Then he moved around in front of me and sat down, cutting his distance from me to about half a tail's length. "Anyway, my luck went south, so I decided to follow it." He chuckled at his own witless joke.

The odor of old tuna on his breath nearly bowled me over. Holding my ground, I glared at him, the fur on my back rising. I determined that there would be *no* encore of past humiliations at the paws of cats like him.

"This neighborhood seems to be a good one. Shoppin' center at the foot of the hill with restaurants and a supermarket. That means lotsa Dumpsters, which means lotsa food. Nice woods for hidin' out in the short-term. In the long run, though, I'm lookin' to start a new life. You know, livin' under the stars is startin' to get a little old. Know anyone who would be interested in takin' me in?" He leaned toward me.

"Not I, certainly. I already have an estate here. I have three staff, the run of the entire household, and a suite of rooms all to myself. I've seen your kind before. You see a chap like me and take advantage, so I'd appreciate it if you'd move along."

"Whooaaa! Man, how'd you score that gig?"

"I beg your pardon?"

"I mean, how did you come up with such a great deal?"

"Well, it hasn't been easy, but through hard work and perseverance, things have worked out quite nicely."

He laughed.

Why did these hoodlums always laugh? No respect for their betters.

"Hard work?" he mocked. "You don't know the first thing about hard work. I can tell just by lookin' atcha." His lip curled, revealing a sharp fang.

"My dear sir, you have been the very definition of *rude* during the entire course of this meeting. Don't make *me* do something *you'll* regret."

We each took a step forward, bringing us nose to nose. I pinned him with my fiercest look; a growl began low in my throat, rising, forming into a hiss. All of his slick, hail-fellow-well-met good humor evaporated, and he returned the low growl. Our fates hung in the balance. I widened my eyes, arched my back, and twitched my well-bristled tail. I was duty bound to protect my estate.

He barely flinched. But in that briefest flicker, all fight seemed to flee from him. He backed away and then loped into the woods behind the townhouse, doubtless terrified.

With the enemy thus routed, I strolled back to my original resting place. Mama would surely be proud if she could see me.

I relaxed, smoothed my fur, and swallowed my ire. It was early autumn, but the midafternoon sun was getting a bit warm. I retired under a shrub in a soft, cool nest of old pine needles and, confident of my position as defender of the estate, slept peacefully through the remainder of the day and into the early evening.

Rusty Hurdman striding toward me ... a spring in his step ... young ruffian. What was he up to now? Hadn't I sent him packing? Tired, so tired ... couldn't get my eyes open ... coming closer, closer ... What? ... Chewing on my ear ... Ouch!

This was no dream at all!

Before I could form another thought or rise from my temporary bed, Rusty sprang fully upon me. I strained to get up into a better position to ward off his attack. But he held me firm as he continued to chomp on my ear.

Now fully awake and thus able to take full stock of my predicament, my adrenaline surged with outrage and fear. I rolled over onto the ruffian. A young cat, he was hard hitting and brawny, and as I was neither, I had to depend on my weight and wits. The rolling maneuver turned out as I had hoped, and I incapacitated him.

"*Rreooouw!* Hey, Fat Boy, get offa me!" he squealed. "Yo mama must feed you too many cream puffs. Yo mama, yo daddy, yo gray-headed granny. Yo mama, yo daddy, yo gray-headed granny."

As he chanted this foul rap, I thought of Mama with her bad accent, her wonderful cuisine, and our common interests, me being chief among them. I thought of my grandmamma, who was a distant memory. I thought of the Alpha Male, and though I did not want to grow up to be like him—that is, go to work every day—he *was* the other male authority around the estate.

"See here, you vile hoodlum," I hissed. "I will release you when I am good and ready! And I will thank you to leave my family out of this."

My indignation gave me the strength to lift up my entire weight and drop it down on him in what I hoped would be a death blow.

Though his breath was nearly gone, he did manage to slither out from under me in two great surges of weasel-like strength. At least he had no more breath to speak. After turning to deliver one final glare, he scurried off into the woods by the pond.

Hmph! *Serves you right.*

But my victory-induced giddiness was short-lived. I was breathing heavily. As the adrenaline subsided, I felt intense pain in my ear where he had chewed it. What had that thug done to me? Without Mama or the Alpha Male to tend to me, it was impossible to know. I limped back toward the courtyard wall. He had taken a bite out of my shoulder. I needed to find some way to scale that wall to get behind its relative safety and away from Hurdman, should he decide to return.

Fortunately, the wall is built into the side of a hill, making the first portion of it much easier to jump to than the lower portion. I gauged even the least possible distance, however, with great care. My shoulder was killing me. Thank heavens, I made it on the first jump. I certainly did not need a sore backside to go with my sore shoulder and ear.

Within the safety of the courtyard, I picked idly at the food Mama had left before her departure. A lone fly transferred his attention from my food to my wounded ear. I batted him away and lapped from my water bowl, grateful that it was relatively cool. I then sought my favorite camellia bush, settled myself as comfortably as possible, and began to lick my wounds in what was now the darkness of night.

What a pretty pass things had come to: nobility in paw-to-paw combat with a common hooligan. Yet I had sent him packing, hadn't I? As I licked my wounds further, I began to feel in the same league with Churchill, Lord Nelson, and William the Conqueror. I had survived. Yes, I had fallen into the pit and prevailed by my own brawn and the hand of Providence.

But oh, my poor ear. I could feel it drooping and my own blood flowing. As a stab of pain jolted me, I had to wonder, where was "God's perfect protection" that Mama often spoke about? Apparently it didn't mean I wasn't going to get pounded on now and then. Like Daniel, I had emerged from the lion's den. But unlike Daniel, I had sustained grievous injuries. No, God had not chosen to close the mouth of the beast I had just dealt with. But then I wasn't Daniel, either, was I? Who was I to tell God what he could and could not open or close?

My disjointed thoughts drifted back to my long-ago stay at Megan's, then to Pet Day and the lessons I had learned about pain and inconvenience, fame and conquest, doors opening, doors closing. Ha! The pains of Pet Day were *nothing* compared to those of this day. After batting away the returning fly's attempt to feast on my wounds, exhaustion overtook me and I fell into a coma of sleep until morning.

The following few days or so—I lost track—passed in a haze of discomfort and Brad's indifference as my wounds remained unattended. I suppose it was partly my fault. As he dropped a scoop of food into the bowl and filled my water dish from the garden hose, I remained under the camellia bush. But in watching him from my leafy cover, I could see that it mattered not one iota to him that I did not make my presence known upon his arrival. As the courtyard gate snapped shut behind him, I limped forth for nourishment and then returned to my resting place, drifting in and out of sleep on a sea of pain. Who knew when my family would return?

"Laddiieee! Laaaaadiiiieeeee! Here, kitty, kitty!"

I awoke from a fitful sleep to realize with great relief that Mama, the Alpha Male, and the Child were home. Hearing the sliding glass door scrape along its track, I managed to stagger forth from under the camellia bush. I squinted into the bright sunlight.

"Oh, Laddie, what happened?" cried Mama as she enfolded me into her arms and kissed me between my ears.

"Laddie, are you okay?" the Child chimed in at her mother's side, her eyes full of worry.

I pulled back and couldn't stop a low, irritated growl from escaping. The ear area was the *last* place I wanted to be touched at that moment.

"I'm sorry, Laddie," Mama crooned. "Tell me all about it."

Oh, if you only knew, Mama — that foul Hurdman character and the things he said about you. I defended your honor.

The Alpha Male stood overhead, displaying a certain detached interest. "Looks like he got his behind kicked. Wonder who did it."

"Look at his ear. We need to get that cleaned up." Mama's voice rose as she shot an exasperated glance at the Alpha Male.

The Alpha Male reached over and patted me gently on my back. "Sorry, big boy. Looks like you've been through it. Let's get you taken care of."

That's more like it.

They proceeded to swab my ear with rubbing alcohol. Not only did it feel like a branding iron, but Mama complained that I *smelled*. Goodness, what was she expecting after an encounter with that foul brute? Chanel No. 5?

All this ministering to my aching body irritated me so that I felt my temper rising. But I knew that it all must be done for my welfare, so I remained patient, neither biting nor scratching. I reminded myself that I must not sink to Rusty Hurdman's level, no matter how painful or inconvenient.

"There, Laddie. All done," Mama cooed.

Finally.

I limped into the estate. Mama had moved my bowls back inside and filled them with fresh food and water. After this satisfying luncheon, I sought the comfort of my suite. I nestled into the pillows and, freed from the anxiety of possible assault, anticipated a long, dreamless sleep.

Just as I was about to drop off, I heard Uncle Romie's voice upstairs. Oh, would this nightmare *never* end?

"I'm glad it was a good trip."

All right, you've said your pleasantries. Now, go.

Then I heard Aunt Lu's concerned, dulcet tones. "Really? Oh, where is he?"

I heard their muted footsteps on the carpeted stairs leading down to my suite. Perhaps I could take a bit more sympathy.

"Handsome, what happened?" Aunt Lu cried.

I settled my gaze on her and chuffled as she gave me a kiss between my ears. Watch that ear, Aunt Lu, watch that ear.

Mama was my spokesperson. "You remember I told you about that orange cat who's been hanging around? The one who was looking in the sliding glass door the other night? I have a feeling it was him."

"Well, Laddie is our wounded warrior, protecting our honor and his," Aunt Lu crooned in her best Southern-lady tones.

"More like some redneck fightin' over a woman." Laughter erupted from Mama.

I shot her a sharp look. Then I turned my head to see Uncle Romie standing in the doorway of my bedroom, arms folded across his chest, grinning.

I glared at him, my damaged ear throbbing. He always thought the worst of me, never gave me the credit I deserved. There simply was no explaining *anything* to him where I was concerned. Aunt Lu had tried countless times. Oh, the pain—my ear, Uncle Romie. I couldn't decide which was worse. Fortunately, he finally retreated to engage the Alpha Male in conversation— something about football scores.

But memoir writing is nothing if not an exercise in seeking perspective; that is, looking back on one's life and seeing the forest as well as the trees, the big picture as well as the small details. So, while Uncle Romie's comment was tactless and crude, it did bring home the fact that prophecy can come from the most unlikely places.

Indeed, as it so happened, Uncle Romie would be partly right.

CHAPTER 20

Love, Bad Weather, and Other Trials

Strolling down the sidewalk during another one of my exiles to the out-of-doors, I was startled by a feminine voice behind me. I stopped and turned around.

"Now, if that's not good-lookin', then I don't know what is!" she meowed.

Nothing flashy about her, but she had a way with words. A simple black-and-gray short-haired tabby, she wore a plain white ascot around her neck. Her stripes were not nearly as crisp and distinct as mine, and she was obviously a stray, that most common of common cats, average in looks and form. But there was still something intriguing about her as she sauntered toward me, her gently curving tail heralding a friendly hello.

Her name was Honey. Her eastern North Carolina accent was like my Aunt Lu's. And her demeanor was kind, warm, and accepting, reminding me of Gertie, though she was much younger. We fell into easy conversation that first day, and our rendezvous soon became regular, as I found myself eagerly anticipating my daily afternoon strolls to meet up with her.

Oh, Honey knew that I could never give her the things of her girlhood dreams—a home of her own, a family, material goods— yet it seemed not to matter to her. She seemed content just to be with me and enjoy endless walks and wanderings by the pond, in the woods behind the estate, down the tidy sidewalks in front of the townhouses.

Honey had been born on an American air base in Germany, but a pilot stationed at Seymour Johnson AFB in eastern North Carolina smuggled her as a kitten into the United States. This faithless captain who'd brought her to America soon tired of finding someone to watch over her when he was frequently called away on missions.

He gave her to a truck driver who hauled vegetables to the farmer's market in Raleigh. Honey, weary from all the travel, alighted from the cab one day at the market, never to return to the trucker.

"It liked to wear me out," she said. "All that back and forth. So I just decided to find out what it would be like on the other side of the fence. The trucker was a very kind man. He always left the truck runnin' with the AC on when he had to leave me to unload. I sometimes wonder whether he got worried over losin' me, but a cat's gotta do what a cat's gotta do."

"Yes, quite," I agreed.

We complemented each other perfectly: I, handsome, intelligent, controlling; and she, earthy, attractive, with a charming touch of the fishwife; this last reminding me a bit of Mama before she's had her morning coffee. And I identified immediately with her sense of adventure and perseverance as well as her connection to trucking as I recalled my long-ago truck ride to Raleigh.

She gave me an affectionate head nudge. "I've never met a cat like you before, Laddie. Bein' noble and all. But I guess you've already figured out that bein' noble don't carry a whole lot of weight around here."

"Yes, you're right. The only thing it's created for me here in the States is headache and mockery." I heaved a sigh.

"Well, it looks like you've landed on your feet, all the same. Hey, I know we've only known each other for a couple of months, but do you think your humans would be interested in takin' me in too?"

My heart skipped a beat. "Honey, this is a bit sudden."

"I know, Laddie, but I think you and I could have a real good partnership. Yes, I know there are certain things we would miss, but the only thing I don't think I could bear to miss is *you*."

Dumbfounded, I stared at her and flicked my tail nervously. My mind raced with questions. How would this benefit me? Would Mama and Aunt Lu still love me best? Would they even *like* Honey? If Mama frowned on one vet bill, what would she think of two? Honey wanted to stay with me, despite my slight shortcomings. I was on the downside of middle age, and this might be my last chance for a mate. Did I really want one? All was confusion. Yet one more look at Honey and all my doubts disappeared.

"Dearest," I began, "I will speak with estate management and get back to you within a couple of days."

"All right. Let's meet by the pond day after tomorrow."

"No, meet me here tomorrow and I will present you to Mama and the Alpha Male. They manage the estate for me, but newcomers are subject to their approval, so pour on your charm, darling. They will take another day to decide, then I shall come for you."

The next day, Honey and I were to meet in front of the estate at about the time the Alpha Male would be returning from work. As Mama was cooking dinner, I sniffed the kitchen aromas with appreciation and slipped down from the armchair onto the Turkish rug without a sound. Soon all of this would be Honey's and mine if things went according to plan. I would raise her from her common depths, and she would keep me magnificently humble.

I found Honey hiding behind the shrub in the front of the townhouse. As the Alpha Male started up the walk, she made her entrance. I greeted her by touching her nose with mine.

The Alpha Male opened the door to the estate. He glanced briefly back at us, then did a double take. "Laddie, what's the matter with you? You hate other cats."

I moved to sit at the side of my beloved, our shoulders touching. With so much at stake, I wore my most humble and pleading expression for the Alpha Male: head up, ears high, gazing at him with wide-eyed politeness.

By this time, Mama had come to the door. She gave the Alpha Male a welcome peck and then looked down on Honey and me. "Who's this?" she asked.

"I think Laddie has a girlfriend," the Alpha Male observed.

How perceptive of him. I gave Mama my best adoring gaze.

"I think he wants to keep her," she said.

"We'll think about it. Let's see if she hangs around."

Honey and I exchanged hopeful glances.

I walked her to the edge of the woods behind the townhouse. "I shall come for you at this same time tomorrow. Wait for me here, dearest."

"Bye, Laddie. See ya then."

Tomorrow dawned and I waited nervously all day. I even sacrificed one of my longer naps. Finally, the Alpha Male came home. "Where's your sweetie, big boy?" he asked.

I looked up at him and chuffled as he leaned down to give my jaw an affectionate scratch. He finished with an encouraging pat on my head and turned to enter the estate. This was my cue to go to the edge of the woods where I knew Honey would be waiting. I ambled across the lawn, not wanting to appear too eager to give her the good news. I knew she was watching from somewhere. I arrived at the exact spot where yesterday we had parted.

No Honey. *Well, she'll be along shortly,* I assured myself. Obviously, she was just reasonably delayed.

I waited. Then I searched the woods, sniffing the breeze, trying to catch her scent. Still no Honey. The sun was dropping toward the horizon. It would be dark soon.

I returned to the front of the estate, increasingly worried over her nonappearance. I barely noticed that rain was falling in large drops, making pinging noises on the glass storm door as the wind increased. The sky had turned a peculiar shade of yellow-green. A chill ran down my spine, but not because it was cold. Something wasn't right. I trudged up the front steps.

Mama was there to meet me and opened the door for me. "Thank goodness you're here, Laddie!" she exclaimed. "There's a bad storm passing through. A tornado touched down in Cary."

Then she bustled off to the kitchen. I sniffed the air. It smelled like her excellent oven-fried chicken, but I couldn't muster much interest.

I glanced at the television screen. Cary is a transplant-filled, posh young city to the west. I thought of that transplanted Yankee, Rusty. Well, Cary could fly away in the wind, as far as I was concerned. And if west Raleigh flew away, too, what did it matter? Where was Honey? That was all I could think of. Was she ill? Had she met with some violent end? I had warned her of the dangers of crossing Wycliff Road.

Flopping down in the living room, I watched the crawler on the bottom of the screen: dime-size hail, winds gusting to sixty-five miles per hour, possible power losses. Then the weatherman cut in, reporting with thinly veiled disappointment that the tornado in Cary had touched down in an open field, and there had been no property damage or injuries. He then brightened as he reminded the viewing audience that there remained a tornado watch in effect till 10:00 p.m. ". . . and now back to regular programming."

The entertainment segment of the local news resumed. Now there was something not to be missed. Having nothing better to do, I settled down with my chin on my paws. The interviewer was talking to some '80s hair band who was playing the PNC Arena that night. She spoke to the front man, a vile-looking middle-aged Brit with orange spandex pants and frightful hair. He was in desperate need of a new stylist. I thought again of Rusty and his tawdry orange coat.

Wait. I quickly got to my feet. Who was that sitting on his lap? My ears flew back and my tail twitched. It was Rusty, on TV, being cosseted by said hair band member! I hissed at the screen. Well, that suits him perfectly. They were *made* for each other. I mentally wished them the best in their livid orange life together and groomed my paw as the interview continued. The camera moved to the lead guitarist, who rattled on about the heat in Raleigh and his fear of tornadoes. Ha-ha. Then the interviewer asked about his "feline friend." As I continued licking my paws, I considered that *friend* was not a word I would use to describe Rusty.

I looked back to the TV. My heart stopped. A close-up of *Honey's* face filled the screen.

My thoughts were as tangled as the blowing branches outside the living room window. *Rusty and Honey, picked up as strays by an '80s hair band. My broken heart. Their bad taste.*

It had never occurred to me that *Rusty* — of all things! — could be the cause of Honey's no-show. How could she do this to me?

Lightning blazed followed by a tremendous boom that set the windows to rattling.

Wrapping up the segment, the reporter urged viewers to come out to the PNC tonight … blah, blah. Then they cut to a commercial. I wandered in a daze into the kitchen, sniffing idly while Mama worked. Flopping on the Turkish rug, I remained lost in thought, enveloped in a haze of self-pity and disbelief over Honey's betrayal. The wind continued to whip the trees outside the kitchen window and green leaves flew by in a wandering, tortured dance that mirrored my state of mind. At last, I raised my head and sniffed.

Hmm ...

That chicken smelled divine. Mama pulled it out of the oven. It looked just as good. I prepared myself for what I would get and groomed my paws again, feeling my energy returning.

David had been taken in by beauty. Solomon by the exotic. Me? Flattery. Furthermore, if Honey could be lured away that quickly by so crass an interloper as Rusty Hurdman, well, this was something best discovered sooner rather than later. I paused to observe Mama and reflected further that she was most assuredly a much better cook as well.

I waited patiently for my portion of oven-fried chicken, relaxed and in control.

And at least the lead guitarist had a British accent.

CHAPTER 21

Imprisonment

Though the years were rolling by agreeably enough, I was starting to feel my age a bit, an ache in my hips from time to time, a decrease in my superior agility. I once heard an athletic, injury-prone friend of Mama's declare, "After twenty-five, it's all patch 'n' seal." This startled me a bit since, at that time, I had been in my early forties in human years. Then again, I'd never heard anyone accuse me of being athletic ... on purpose, anyway.

On this bright summer morning, I was feeling particularly inquisitive. Having slept in a bit, I'd completed my morning estate rounds later than usual. Thoroughly refreshed and ready for whatever the rest of the day would bring, it occurred to me that, even after all these years, I had never visited some courtyards in the neighborhood, those that were a good deal more distant than I generally traveled. Today I would correct this oversight.

I strolled across the common area lawn, its wideness seeming to increase with my age. Making my way across the grass, I paused every so often to rest and sniff idly to determine what the fresh breeze might carry. Fortunately, no other cats were about. May I be frank? I was *through* with my species. Only dread and disappointment were to be had from them, and the years were passing happily without them, thank you very much.

Reflecting on this, I ambled down the narrow wooded footpath leading to the courtyards in question. I passed Jil's courtyard. Remember Jil, the caviar neighbor? The memory of that sumptuous, forbidden snack gave me pause. Looking up through her living room window, I spotted her cat lounging on the back of a couch and glaring down at me. I didn't know his name. As a house cat, he never ventured outside, poor creature. His mouth formed a hiss. What else could I expect from a cat? I ignored him.

Turning my attention back to the footpath, I passed several vacant courtyards, their adjoining townhouses either for sale or seasonally emptied of humans, and then came upon a wrought iron gate. Peering through the bars, I spotted a wall fountain, its water glittering in the late morning sunlight. The garden was just as nice as Mama's, but it reminded me of an Italian piazza, with its gurgling fountain, brick walls covered with fragrant jasmine vines, and hanging baskets filled with cascading pink and red bougainvillea. The whole setting was irresistible, beckoning me within to find a place of respite for a long nap. Though further from the estate than I had ever ventured, I was confident that I would be able to hear Mama's call when she arrived home from work at midday to summon me for my luncheon.

So I put my head through the bars of the gate. But when I got to my thriving midsection—another result of my advancing years—I was stuck, halfway in and halfway out. I did manage to make it through, but not before acquiring from one of the bars a sizeable scratch on my girth. I turned to groom the area, a slight taste of blood on my tongue. No matter. Heaven knows, I'd certainly suffered worse, a fleeting thought of my battle with Rusty Hurdman coming to mind.

The brick pavers felt cool on my paws as I glanced about for a napping place, which I spotted under a Japanese maple. I lowered myself upon a plush carpet of green moss. The shade was delicious on what promised to be another horribly hot day.

As I congratulated myself on my discovery and made myself comfortable, I listened intently, as yet unfamiliar with my surroundings. The burble of falling water in the fountain conjured mental pictures of Rome as my eyes closed.

A shady piazza ... a small café ... succulent seafood and a fine, bittersweet tiramisu redolent with chocolate and espresso-dipped lady fingers ... heavenly whipped mixture of cream, mascarpone, and eggs — Mama makes it the same way. "What's not to like?" she honks cheerfully. The Alpha Male and the Child nod in earnest agreement ... I wait not very patiently for mine. Dear Mama. Dear desserts. Dear Mama —

"Laadieeeee ... Laaaaadieeeee ... Here, kitty, kitty!"

I awoke with a start, hearing Mama's call, which was far more distant than I would have thought. After such a lovely dream about food, I was ravenous, not to mention very thirsty. So I got up and loped to the gate. I then stuck my head through, but when I got to my girth—especially the scratched area—well, I couldn't pass through this time. I barely managed to back up and free myself. I tried more than one bar. No success. What's more, the scratch was now quite painful and irritated as a result of the repeated tries.

By this time, Mama had stopped calling, likely assuming that some unanticipated estate business had detained me. I let loose with a good wail, beginning with my distinct bass and crescendoing to a good old-fashioned yowl. I repeated this several times to no avail. A lower class of cat would have fallen to panic. No sense at all in wearing myself out, so I again sought my green mossy carpet in the shade for another extended nap. Besides, I reasoned further, the townhouse owner would be home soon, discover me with my identifying collar, and take me back to Mama.

Oh, what's this?

Against the courtyard wall in the bright sunlight was an attractive wrought iron box, the bars of which matched the courtyard gate. Now empty, it looked like it was used to store firewood in the winter months. I walked over and gave it a sniff. Its lid was wide open, beckoning further inspection. Curious as to what its interior was like, I jumped up over the side. I've still got it. I can still jump with the best of—

Crash!!

Just barely missing my tail, the lid came down with a heavy metallic clank followed by a click of the latch. I startled at the noise and looked up. I knew at once that I was locked in. I glanced around me but spotted nothing intriguing. Funny how something that seems so attractive can be so unpleasant once you actually experience it.

A yellow paper taped to the French doors leading into the townhouse caught my eye. It read: THANKS FOR DELIVERING THE NEW DISHWASHER ON TUESDAY AS REQUESTED. PLEASE SEE MY NEIGHBOR AT 2816 GLENFALL. SHE WILL LET YOU IN. I APPRECIATE IT, STEVE.

My stomach dropped like a stone. This fellow would *not* be home soon. He was out of town, and his neighbor, who lived blocks away, would not be coming to let anyone in for *three whole days*. My thoughts darted to all of those empty courtyards I had passed that separated me from human help. This meant I needed to consider how on earth to get out of this prison of my own making, which was in full sun and getting hotter by the minute.

I peered through the bars into the darkened basement beyond the French doors and watched a large lava lamp in the corner calmly burping blue globs. Two things occurred to me: this Steve fellow had nauseating taste in home accessories, and I did *not* feel calm. I began to pace, my ears back and panic rising with each step. I glanced up toward Jil's townhouse. It had disappeared from view.

What was I to do? I paced for what seemed like hours in the hot sun, thoughts of deliverance churning in my brain, having no idea from what quarter a savior might appear, if any savior appeared at all. I rested from time to time, the day passing in an intermittent frenzy of heat and high anxiety. Finally, I could pace no more as exhaustion overtook me. I began to pant—good grief, almost like a dog. Mercifully, about midafternoon the sun lowered behind a tall tree and then, finally at dusk, the courtyard wall. Still breathing heavily, I lowered myself onto the metal bottom of the box. Some dead leaves provided a bit of shield from the heat. I was now cool enough to pass into sleep. But it brought no rest, only vivid dreams that mirrored my present predicament, nightmares in which I was no longer in my cage but roaming the neighborhood—now transformed into a desolate dustbowl—unable to find my family, water, or food.

When I awoke, the first stars of the night sky twinkled overhead. I heard both Mama and the Child, still distant, calling me in earnest. They had no idea where I was. I'd had no food or water since early morning. At least the terrible sun was now gone, but my throat was now absolutely parched. The falling water of the fountain, which had been so charming, now taunted me. My Roman piazza had turned into the Tower of London.

My tongue felt cottony in my mouth. I resumed pacing about the cage, more slowly this time like some doomed circus animal, still searching for a way out but knowing there was none. The only way out was the way in. I batted uselessly at the top of the box with my paw. My only hope was to muster enough strength to raise my voice again in another cry for help.

As I lingered over the thought of raising my voice, I recalled Catarina, my opera-singing mother, who had abandoned me all those years ago. This gave me some inspiration. I let forth with a series of yowls worthy of the Von Caterwaul name. Then I lowered myself onto the bottom of the box, completely spent.

The automatic uplights in the courtyard flickered on, outlining the fountain's falling water and bringing my surroundings into what should have been a soothing, lovely twilight.

Then I saw it—slithering out from under an uplit bush. Instinctively, I crouched low and watched unblinkingly as its length continued to present itself. At last, the end of it emerged from the shrubs, a copperhead snake that looked about three feet long. Its tube-like body hugged the ground as it slid its slow, sinuous way in my direction.

I was almost too weak to think, yet I instinctively assessed my ability to defend myself. The bars of the wood box offered full access to the serpent, but no avenue of escape to me—a perfect death chamber. I grimly recalled Mama's admonition to take heed of these ghastly reptiles, her proud words that I was stealthy and could surely spot any snake first and thus escape. She'd had no worries about me. Oh, if she were only here!

What was I to do? What *could* I do? Nothing. I was dazed, exhausted, weak from lack of water; and now this hideous, venomous creature was headed straight at me.

My life flashed before me—being whacked off a cruise ship into New York Harbor, almost going to the shelter, the Schroders rescuing me, the now-empty victory over Rusty Hurdman, losing Honey, being done with my species, and now losing the Schroders and all I held dear.

Was this how it was all going to end?

The snake continued its belly march toward me, its skin emitting a dull sheen in the courtyard lights whose glow spotlighted the death scene playing out. It stopped outside the wood box, its triangular head less than a foot from me and well within killing distance. It tasted the air with its forked tongue.

Did it savor my fear?

I crouched in defense and flattened my ears, the sound of my heart pounding in them. Surely the serpent could hear it. The snake's tongue flicked, its mechanical stare fixed upon me. His body retreated slightly into an S. For a split second, I thought the snake was departing. Then it was clear. It was preparing to strike.

Oh Jesus, please save me.

CHAPTER 22

Rescue — And Then Some

E xcited barks broke through my fear.

The snake heard them, too, as it froze and turned its head in the direction of the noise. I detected human voices among the barking. The sounds grew louder as they drew closer.

The snake slithered toward the gate, its head disappearing first, followed by its seemingly endless body until the last inch vanished, presumably to the distant, swampy woods from whence it had come. In all my life, I was *never* so relieved to see the last of something. I yowled again in earnest, releasing pent-up terror along with a renewed determination to summon help.

A moment later, Mildred the terrier appeared at the gate. Oh, talk about being relieved! For once, I was actually glad to see her high-strung, noisy little self. And not just glad, but *thrilled*. She sniffed the ground outside the gate with such intensity that I thought she might choke on the dust. There was no question — she knew what threat had just passed. She raised her head high and stared directly at me, her brown eyes full of courage and care. Her tiny barrel chest swelled, most likely with indignation at the thought of the deadly interloper, and her mouth hardened into a grim line.

Then she set to barking anew for all she was worth, clearly indicating that she recognized my desperate need for liberation and was determined to raise a ruckus until help arrived. Every so often she stopped to smile encouragingly at me and wag her stubby little tail.

Presently, I heard the Alpha Male's voice. "... and thanks for letting us know you heard him."

"You're welcome," Jil said. "I had just arrived home from work and was on my way back out the door to dinner. But then I remembered I had to water my plants downstairs. I heard Mildred barking. She was really the one who alerted me. Then I heard this awful yowling from somewhere on the other side of my courtyard wall. I walked several doors down and there sat Laddie in Steve's wood box. Oh, he was having a perfectly royal fit."

Yes, and what would you do?

The Alpha Male reached down, and with a metallic clank, he released the latch on the wood box and stepped back, clearly waiting for me to jump out.

I arose on wobbly legs, exhausted and shaky from a lack of sustenance and an overdose of adrenaline-laced trauma. I wanted to jump out and meow in complaint and relief, *Good heavens, what took you so long?* Physically, though, I wasn't certain I could even make the jump.

But something else held me back. I was all at once ashamed of myself. Call it sudden humility stemming from the knowledge that I was no longer as resourceful as I used to be. Call it regret that I had only myself to blame and not some other cat or human, regret over my own stupidity and arrogance, acting as if I owned every place my paw touched, wandering into places where I had no right to be. Call it anything you like, but I was *embarrassed* to have to be rescued.

I slowly paced about in my prison, trying to ignore them. By this time, Mama, Aunt Lu, and the Child had arrived. I sniffed the air in their direction, smelling deliverance but still unwilling — maybe unable? — to accept it.

It comes from living in a nest of Bible readers, but one of Mama's favorite verses came to mind unbidden: "He has rescued us from the dominion of darkness and brought us into the kingdom of the Son he loves." She loves it for the sound of it, the bold lyricism that underscores complete liberation from an otherwise conquering force, a deliverance not worked for but granted *freely*. Yes, that was it! I just needed to accept this gift of rescue. No, I could *not* accomplish rescue by myself, save myself, and stroll home as if nothing had happened. But that's the definition of rescue. Someone does it *for* you.

A sudden burst of energy, propelled me upward to freedom. I made a successful landing on the other side of my prison wall.

The Child picked me up immediately and hugged me close. I didn't even mind. Mama, Aunt Lu, and the Alpha Male gathered around, talking among themselves and generally emitting joyful sighs and words of relief over finding what had been lost.

Mildred's humans presently arrived on the scene and the Schroders quickly brought them up-to-date on Mildred's heroics. They scooped her up, held her close, and concurred with the Schroders' and Aunt Lu's assessment that Mildred was "extraordinary." I didn't even balk at that conclusion, as Mildred and her family strolled happily back to their home.

Then I caught sight of another person coming around the corner of the row of townhouses. Surely not him, striding toward us and smiling with — dare I even say it? — obvious relief that I had been found, safe and unharmed. Of all people, Uncle Romie spoke no harsh words. No sarcastic humor. Not a word.

The Child beamed. "Laddie, I'm so glad we found you!" She put her forehead against mine.

Abandoning myself to the spirit of the moment, I gave her an affectionate lick on the cheek.

Aunt Lu sniffed. "What would I do without you, Handsome?"

Mama kissed me between the ears, then dabbed her eyes.

The Alpha Male looked like he wanted to say something, but only swallowed hard and gave me an awkward pat on the head.

We made our way to the front of the townhouse row and across the wide lawn toward our front door.

But of course, Uncle Romie could not hold back forever. He seemed bursting to say something untoward, which he did. First, something about my having interrupted a perfectly good dinner. Then, still grinning, he added, "I can see why y'all were afraid he was dead, 'cause you *know* that's the only way he would miss two meals."

Aunt Lu punched him in the arm, making him wince.

But not even Uncle Romie could offend me now. I was engaged with further thoughts about my deliverance. I had already established that I was through with my species. Jil and Mildred were instrumental in my rescue — Jil, a human who didn't even like me, and Mildred, a *dog* about whom I had had many unkind thoughts. Yet I was wholly grateful to both of them!

Did this mean that wonderful, necessary things can come from previously unthinkable sources? That I shouldn't be so quick to bang the gavel of judgment? And that maybe, just maybe, I should be willing to *extend* mercy as well as receive it?

Furthermore, was it possible I was learning humility as a result of having been humbled? Almost to death? Oh, there was much to contemplate.

Mama, murmuring words of comfort, carried me downstairs to my fresh food and water, then returned to the happy chatter upstairs. My dinner tasted especially good — even the Hairball Lite — in the cool safety of my basement home. I took my last bite and retreated to my comfortable bed. As I leaped up and cleared the side of it, I thankfully remembered that I was no longer jumping out of a prison but hopping up to take a nice long nap in the safety of my room. I lowered my chin onto the down comforter, closed my eyes, and reflected on Mama's recent words of comfort: *Laddie, don't just accept rescue. Be thankful for it, enjoy it, and rest on it.*

Wise words, indeed. And, as you well know, I never refuse an invitation to rest.

EPILOGUE

It is a Saturday afternoon in autumn, and raindrops are pattering against the window. Mama, Aunt Lu, and the Child are watching *Becoming Jane*, all three of them fans of a good British costume drama, bless them. Mama has just returned to the living room, bringing glasses filled with iced tea and a big bowl of warm popcorn. The only thing that interests me about popcorn is the butter, but I'm very old now and my hips hurt all of the time, so I will just stay where I am, curled up in the sage-green velveteen chaise, dozing to the sounds of the movie, their conversation, and low laughter.

Later, Mama will carry me to my food bowl, as it hurts to use the stairs now. She could just move the food and water upstairs, but she likes to carry me and I really don't mind.

The weather has turned cooler. Another school year for the Child has begun. Dinnertime chatter is about sixth grade. Yes, it seems as if it were only yesterday when she was that tiny, chubby-fisted grabber. There are many things for which a cat can be grateful in this life, and high on the list is the fact that children get older. And with age, she has become a comforter and carrier on a par with Mama.

Aunt Lu left that multinational bank after over twenty years of matchless performance in the field of marketing and client services. However, she left not for more prestige or money, but to work for next to nothing in a ministry that exists to encourage and mentor business women. Hmm. Ministry? I had my doubts at first. But she seems to enjoy it; she has a new spring in her step. And she has turned cheerfully cheap. Oh, did I say cheap? I meant *frugal*, just like Mama.

Actually, I do identify with Aunt Lu. I, too, lost money and a title, but in losing these, I found, well, I suppose I must call it a rebirth, a whole new life of love and contentment with others so unlike me. Really, what's a cat to do but accept and enjoy it? And I often reflect in quieter moments—of which I now have many here in my old age—that money can buy a house, but it can't buy a home. It can buy things, but it can't buy love. A title can give you an estate in the country, but it can't give you a place to belong.

Yes, I've endured cataclysms of change. Remember Job? Like him, I lost my family and home. Then God gave me different, better ones. I lost my wealth too. But unlike Job, mine was not restored. Yet I feel wealthier than ever.

The Alpha Male still leaves the house faithfully each morning, Monday through Friday, to perform his income-production tasks for the estate. He has commented recently that he feels like all he does is chase his tail. I sympathize. I do the same when I get a rare burst of fleeting energy. Mama and Aunt Lu say my tail chasing is due to encroaching dementia. The Alpha Male says his is due to the difficulty in recruiting good help, which can induce dementia. And that's another thing I've learned: one can never have too much good help.

I sometimes enter a room and forget why I am there, but Mama and Aunt Lu are in middle age and they do the same, which is comforting. Feline comforts are plentiful, actually, and I do try to be grateful. I still do better with entitlement than gratitude. Perhaps you can relate.

Uncle Romie? Well, wonders abound, especially those of the culinary variety. He has become an amazingly good cook. Not like Mama, of course, but he does make a perfectly acceptable pimento cheese. And he makes a sweet potato tart so light that it can only be described as sublime. He should send the recipe to Maxim's. But I won't be going back to Maxim's. That life is gone now. And Uncle Romie has shown me that true creativity can flourish in the most unlikely of places.

And speaking of wonders, I have become *friends* with Mildred, my Jack Russell terrier neighbor. Can you believe it? Yes, it appears that Jesus still walks on water. Miracles *do* happen. I love my canine neighbor. She often greets me with a happy bark as I make my substantially slower daily rounds. She even once saved me from an obnoxious large yellow Lab. It is good to have a friend who is also a defender. I never extended myself to Mildred before she took part in leading me to rescue. She really has no earthly reason to be my friend, but she is anyway.

Now from the cover of the bushes, as I watch Mildred with her humans, I see something new. Where I used to see a dog, I now see a comrade. Where I used to see senseless hyperactivity, I now recognize energetic joy. Where I used to see a mindless servant, I observe overflowing love for those who take care of her. I don't think I'll ever be exactly like Mildred, any more than she could ever be exactly like me. But she has brought me to the happy conclusion that I'm done with having a family that I look upon as a staff. It's better to have a family. Period.

And I have even had second thoughts about having Mama as my master. Shocking, isn't it? Well, why not? A master who not only takes good care of you, but takes delight in being with you — and goes to great pains to demonstrate that? A master who notices when you've gone missing and goes after you to save your life? It's worth every compromise. Yes, even every act of surrender. Indeed, it is good to have a master.

You just have to pick the right one.

And speaking of masters, ever since I've known Mama, she has seen God as hers, not remote or disinterested but as close as her next breath, living, loving, saving, protecting, and in charge. And if he's in charge of Mama, it must follow that he is in charge of me. And me being in charge? Well, clearly, it's been an ambitious failure, overrated at best and near fatal at worst.

Do you know that Mama has lived in the South for over twenty years now? I've heard her say that it is not like where she was born and grew up. I can certainly relate to that. I've also heard her say that it's been years since she's felt like a transplant, a foreigner, and that when a few of the natives love you, you are home.

Ah yes, a good stretch would do nicely about now. I'll just curl back down into the warmth of my beloved chaise, tail curled about my nose, eyes closing...a fine, slow sigh.

I am home, too.

The End

*I*t wasn't so long ago that we ourselves were stupid and stubborn, dupes of sin ... going around with a chip on our shoulder, hated and hating back. But when God, our kind and loving Savior God, stepped in, he saved us from all that. It was all his doing; we had nothing to do with it. He gave us a good bath, and we came out of it new people, washed inside and out by the Holy Spirit. Our Savior Jesus poured out new life so generously. God's gift has restored our relationship with him and given us back our lives. And there's more life to come – an eternity of life! You can count on this.

– Titus 3:3–8 MSG

Acknowledgments

Lucretia (more frequently known as Lu Ann). While I put the words together, Lu Ann was a cheerleader and encourager extraordinaire over the course of 14 years of picking up and setting aside the manuscript while we both experienced moves, parenting, deaths, lives celebrated and mourned and – Laddie would want us to be honest – procrastinating because we did not know what the heck we were doing. I'm not sure we do now. But Lu Ann laughed at my jokes while we both laughed at the cat. That's a sign of a great friend - someone who laughs, whether or not you're actually funny.

Boy James – a fun feline who made great entertainment for us at his expense. He seldom seemed happy to foot the bill. But I saved him in the same way God saved me. Yes, minus Him, I am the uppity but cluelessly desperate cat.

Our families who restrained their eye-rolling as the writing process went on and on and prayed for, encouraged us, and gave practical help in ways large and small, from grammar to "Write more." Special thanks to Anna, whose imaginative toddler mind and love of books originally inspired Laddie.

Our families of faith in Raleigh, Durham, and Chapel Hill, the joy-filled, wickedly funny, godly men and women who are living proof that God gives us many gifts but two of those oft-overlooked are laughing till it hurts and a sense of humor about yourself. I never knew knowing God could be so much fun. And I used to think those born-again church people were dull.

Erin Brown of the Write Editor who was the first person outside family and friends to meet and love Laddie. She encouraged me and clarified the cat, bringing him to life in ways I never could have, and became a friend in the process.

Richard Fitzpatrick, former BBC sound engineer who captured so well the voice of Laddie for our YouTube video. Uppity with a touch of pathos was what we were looking for. Richard, you delivered. I wish I could speak like you every day.

The folks at EA Books Publishing – Cheri, Bob, Michelle, Amber, Dawn, and Tanya - whose patient professionalism and care made Laddie into a book – and editor Christy Callahan who gave final polish to Laddie's voice and with great forbearance guided low-tech me through the world of Track Changes.

Bret Witter, Juana Mikels, Jodie Berndt, all of whose encouragement and advice on things publishing and writing were so valuable and so much appreciated.

Our Father God for so clearly demonstrating for us through everyday pieces of His world – like pet adoption – his transforming power, compassion, and relentless love for all who believe.

With joy and thanks,
Allison and Lu Ann

In the rustling grass I hear Him pass
He speaks to me everywhere.

– "This is My Father's World" by Maltbie Davenport Babcock

About the Authors

Allison Snyder was raised on a dairy farm in western New York where her fascination with writing and cats began in earnest and never left. She loves to write about pies and cakes too. Her food and pet essays have appeared over the years in *Raleigh News & Observer, The Triangle Dog,* and *The News of Orange County.* She is also a guest blogger (www.plantingcabbages.com) for a cooking school in Chapel Hill, North Carolina, where she works as an assistant chef/instructor for desserts. A French major at North Carolina State University, Allison studied fiction writing there under the late Tim McLaurin. She makes her home in Orange County, North Carolina, with her husband and daughter.

Lucretia Herring is a graduate of North Carolina Wesleyan University and a retired Fortune 500 banking executive. She lives in Raleigh, North Carolina, with her husband. Lu is full of ideas, and Laddie's journey of hope is one of her crazier and more enduring ones. She also enjoys Allison's pets without having to pay any vet bills.

Both authors and their families like to scarf down anything Allison bakes. The authors met in a Bible study at a hotel-gone-church in Raleigh over fifteen years ago and have remained friends ever since.

Made in the USA
Charleston, SC
03 January 2017